"All right. You'd better tell me all about it."
Kelly drew back, eyes grave

Despite the warm sun, a chill raised bumps on Max's forearms. How could she know? He'd stashed the letter deep in the bottom drawer of his office filing cabinet. "What do you mean?"

"You're hiding something," Kelly stated. "You've been acting weird all weekend, guilty and secretive—when you weren't giving me a tumble, that is." She crossed her arms. "Spill it."

At first Kelly thought he would evade this demand for explanations, too. Then before her eyes, Max seemed to shrink from her and turn inward. Her heart sank. Whatever he was hiding must be really bad. He was having an affair. He wanted a divorce. He—

"I have a son."

She stared. She'd heard him speak, but the words had no meaning. "What did you say?"

"I have a son," he repeated.

"That's impossible. Unless," she added with a short, humorless laugh, "one of the twins had a sex change."

"*Kelly.*"

"But it's impossible, Max," she repeated. "We were married right out of high school. How could you have a child I don't know about...."

Dear Reader,

Most romance novels stop at the altar; I've often thought this is where the story of a couple really begins. Some couples, like Kelly and Max Walker, are meant to be together. But even the happiest of families may have secrets that rock the very foundation of a solid marriage.

On her thirteenth wedding anniversary Kelly learns that Max had a son by a liaison previously unknown to her, and their past becomes a lie. When Max, who longs for more children, discovers Kelly is pregnant and contemplating abortion, their future is in jeopardy.

Max wants a son. Kelly wants a life. For a marriage to survive it requires not just love but a willingness to accommodate the needs of a partner who may have different life goals. Is the love that brought Kelly and Max together as teenagers strong enough to transcend their problems and nurture them through their evolving relationship?

Child of Their Vows is my third book about the Hanson sisters of Hainesville, Washington. *Child of His Heart* featured Kelly's elder sister, Erin, and *Child of Her Dreams* was about her younger sister, Geena. Finally it's Kelly's turn to have her story told. I hope you've enjoyed reading about Kelly's, Erin's and Geena's special relationship with one another, and the men they love, as much as I've enjoyed writing about them. I'm going to miss being part of their world!

I love to hear from readers. Please write me at P.O. Box 234, Point Roberts, Washington 98281-0234, or visit me at www.superauthors.com.

Joan Kilby

Child of Their Vows

Joan Kilby

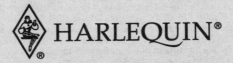

HARLEQUIN®

TORONTO • NEW YORK • LONDON
AMSTERDAM • PARIS • SYDNEY • HAMBURG
STOCKHOLM • ATHENS • TOKYO • MILAN • MADRID
PRAGUE • WARSAW • BUDAPEST • AUCKLAND

ISBN 0-373-71114-X

CHILD OF THEIR VOWS

Copyright © 2003 by Joan Kilby.

This edition published by arrangement with Harlequin Books S.A.

® and TM are trademarks of the publisher. Trademarks indicated with ® are registered in the United States Patent and Trademark Office, the Canadian Trade Marks Office and in other countries.

Visit us at www.eHarlequin.com

Printed in U.S.A.

Child of Their Vows

CHAPTER ONE

"YOU WON'T BE LATE *TONIGHT,* I hope." Max followed Kelly to the front door as she prepared to leave for work.

That today was their thirteenth wedding anniversary seemed to have slipped his wife's ever-practical mind. He, on the other hand, had made romantic plans—a weekend for two at the Salish Lodge, at Snoqualmie Falls, east of Seattle.

"No, I promise," Kelly said absently, slipping her feet into pumps while consulting her "to do" list. "Let's see...dry cleaning, water bill— Oh, this morning I'm showing someone around the Harper house," she interrupted herself to inform Max. "If I make a sale I'll pick up some champagne." She took a pen from the side pocket of her purse and wrote that in with a question mark beside it.

Max leaned forward to breathe in the scent of lavender and vanilla emanating from Kelly's glossy brown shoulder-length hair. He already had a bottle of bubbly chilling in the back of the fridge.

Her gaze still moving over her list, Kelly stood on tiptoes and angled her cheek for a peck from Max. He was aiming for her lips when she burst out, "Omigosh! The laundry," and slipped out of his arms to reverse her steps down the hall.

"*I'll* do that," Max said, irritation puncturing his buoyant mood. He strode after her to stand in the doorway of the laundry room while she sorted whites from colors at whirlwind speed. "Or we could do something really radical and hire a cleaning lady."

"And pay someone for work I can do perfectly well myself? I don't think so." Kelly stuffed the dirty clothes into the washing machine, added detergent and spun the dial. "I promised you when I started working that the housework wouldn't suffer. Besides, I overheard you tell a client you'd have his house design ready this afternoon."

"The girls are waiting in the car for you to take them to school," he reminded her. Kelly's morning route included dropping the twins, Tammy and Tina, at play school, before driving Robyn and Beth over to the elementary school.

"I'm on my way." She edged around him in preparation for the dash to her station wagon.

"Before you enter warp speed..." Max grabbed hold of her shoulders and halted her long enough to plant a kiss on her mouth. "Happy anniversary, Mrs. Walker."

"Anniversary!" Her fingers flew to a mouth rounded in astonishment. "Is it really May 8?"

Max nodded wryly. "All day."

Her arms went around his neck for a quick hug. "Happy anniversary, sweetheart. Why don't we order pizza for the kids tonight and you and I go out to a restaurant."

"Sure you can spare the time?" Max said, poker-faced. Little did Kelly know they would be eating their anniversary dinner in the hotel where they'd spent their honeymoon.

Taking no notice of his sarcasm, she whipped out her list and busily wrote another memo to herself. "Call Nancy to baby-sit."

"I've already talked to Nancy. Now, *go,* before you make the kids late again."

Once she'd left, Max headed for the kitchen and another cup of coffee. He tried to keep a sense of humor about Kelly's attempts to be supermom, *and* career woman, but the long hours she spent at the real estate office took a toll on their family life and had become a constant source of conflict. His patience regarding her promises to slow down were fast running out.

"This weekend better work a little magic on our

marriage,'' he told Billy, a golden retriever, and Flora, a young black Labrador, who dogged his footsteps ever hopeful of treats. ''Because if Kelly and I don't get some loving back in our relationship, we could end up in divorce court instead of having another baby.''

Billy thumped his feathery tail in sympathy, while Flora did her best to make Max feel better by licking his bare toes. Then they scoured the terra-cotta tiles for fallen crumbs missed on earlier forays.

Coffee in hand, Max repaired to his home office. Billy and Flora flopped at his feet beneath the computer and promptly fell asleep as Max went to work on his latest architectural commission; a luxury home on Whidbey Island, near Seattle. Early in his career, Max had drafted plans for everything from garden sheds to business offices, but his real love was innovative home design. He had a small but growing clientele, and if his entry in the prestigious Stonington Award was to win, his career could take a sharp upward turn.

Max didn't glance up from his computer until he heard the familiar rumble of the mailman's truck. Then he rose, stretched and walked down the long gravel driveway to the mailbox, its upright red flag visible between the two big cedar trees that guarded the front of the one-acre property.

As he strolled back to the house, sorting through the bills and flyers, he came upon a letter addressed to him in unfamiliar handwriting. Slowing his pace, he turned over the envelope and saw that the return address was Jackson, Wyoming.

Fourteen years ago he'd spent the summer after high school working on a dude ranch near Jackson. He hadn't thought of the ranch in years, or of Lanni, the vivacious redhead who, with him, had had a job leading trail rides. They'd had a hot fling. The summer had ended. He and Lanni had parted, and he'd returned to Hainesville to marry Kelly, the only woman he'd ever loved.

His hands trembling slightly, Max inserted a finger beneath the flap and ripped open the envelope. Inside was a wallet-size photograph of a young teenage boy and a single page written in a small, very neat hand.

Dear Mr. Walker, My name is Randall and I'm your son.

Cold shock stopped Max in his tracks. Surely this couldn't be happening.... And yet, at some deep level, he'd been waiting thirteen years for this letter.

Maybe you won't want to hear from me, but I had to write. My adoptive parents know I'm contacting you. I have a good home with them and I don't want to intrude on your life—I'd just like to know my bi-

ological father. I hope you understand. And I hope you'll want to meet me, too....

Max lifted his face and gazed blindly into the bright blue sky. *He had a son.*

Like Max, Lanni had only been eighteen. When she'd gotten pregnant her parents had been adamant there would be no marriage or keeping the baby. Nor had he *wanted* to marry her. He'd wanted Kelly.

His and Lanni's baby had been given away at birth; no one had ever told him the baby's gender. Afterward they'd agreed there was no point in keeping in touch. All these years, he'd put the child's existence out of his mind because it hurt too much to think of a son or daughter of his growing up somewhere, without him.

Kelly. He'd never told her about Lanni or the baby he'd fathered. To his shame, he'd always considered it a stroke of undeserved good fortune that she'd never found out.

Despite a breeze, perspiration dampened his hairline. If he wanted to meet Randall he would have to tell her now. But how? And how would she react? With their ongoing marital problems, could they survive the sudden appearance of his child by another woman? He and Kelly had been going together for two years before that summer. He'd already asked her to marry him.

Maybe he shouldn't say anything to her about the boy. Maybe he should throw away the letter without replying, hang on to what he had....

Max turned to the photograph. Randall had straight red hair, severely cut and neatly combed, a smattering of freckles and a solemn smile. Gazing out from behind the chunky frames of his glasses were Max's sky-blue eyes.

So this was his son.

Max loved his daughters with a ferocity and depth that constantly surprised him, and he would cut off both arms rather than hurt them, but...

In the deepest corner of his heart, in a place not even Kelly knew about, he'd always wanted a son. A boy to take fishing and shoot hoops with. A male compadre in a house full of females. A son who would carry on the Walker family name. Was he wrong to want all that? Max didn't think so.

"I'M HOME!" KELLY KICKED OFF her shoes and dumped her purse on the hall table. From the family room at the back of the house she could hear the muffled sound of canned laughter on TV.

She poked her head into Max's office; he wasn't there. Architectural drawings were spread across his drafting table, the goosenecked lamp had been left on and his chair pushed back, as though he'd just stepped out for a moment.

Walking around Tammy's—or was it Tina's?—Barbie dollhouse, Kelly continued on to the family room, drawn by the smell of chili con carne—Max's specialty. She hoped this didn't mean they weren't going out. Max was probably angry, because in spite of her promise, she was late. She swore that this weekend she would make it up to him.

The family room curtains were open, and visible through floor-to-ceiling windows were the twilit river and the forest beyond, and, of course, the extensive flower beds that ringed the lawn. Two pink-sock-clad feet dangled over the side arm of the couch—Beth, glued to her favorite TV show.

Max, his wheat-blond hair gleaming beneath halogen down lights, stood in the kitchen, dicing green peppers on a chopping board. An enormous bouquet of red roses arranged in a vase on the black granite benchtop sent out a faint sweet fragrance.

Max's shoulders had that tight look they got when he was wrestling with a difficult design problem. She hoped he'd been able to finish the drawings for his client's house so he could celebrate their anniversary. God knows, they both needed to set work and responsibilities aside and pay attention to each other for a change.

She dropped her keys on the sideboard and crossed the room to him. "Hi, Max. How was your day?"

"Kelly! I didn't hear you come in."

His upward glance of swiftly concealed guilt startled her. *She* was the one who ought to feel badly. She'd promised she wouldn't be late tonight, and here he was making dinner—that was *her* job—instead of working on whatever problem he'd left on his drafting table.

"Sorry I'm late." She circled one arm around his waist and reached up to remove the forgotten pencil tucked behind his ear. "Did you get your design finished?"

He shook his head and moved away to scrape the green pepper into the pot of chili simmering on the stove. "I called the client and told him it won't be ready until next week."

"I'm really sorry. Thanks for picking up the kids." Damn. She *always* seemed to be apologizing on account of her job. With a sigh, she buried her nose in the roses. "These are gorgeous. Dare I hope they're for me?"

"Of course they're for you."

"You sweetheart. You know what I like."

"I know you're crazy about flowers." He put down the chopping board and pulled her into his arms. Kissed her mouth, then kissed her all over her face. "I love you, Kelly."

"Max! Your hands are wet," she protested, laughing, and slipped out of his embrace. He wasn't usually so passionate at this time of day. And his not being annoyed with her was strange. She gestured to the chili pot. "We were going to order pizza for the kids."

"I thought cooking might clear my head."

"The house design giving you trouble?" She felt both sympathetic and guilty. In the old days, she would have been available for him to bounce ideas off of. Since she'd started working, she had become a source of problems for him instead of solutions.

Max turned away to stir the simmering pot with the wooden spoon he was holding. A tumbler of cola and ice sat on the benchtop beside the stove. "I haven't been able to concentrate on it this afternoon. How did you do with the Harper house?"

Kelly scowled at the surge of frustration his question brought on. "Ray gave me such a hard time afterward. You'd think I was trying to ruin his business."

"What happened?"

She shrugged. "Nothing so terrible. I simply pointed out to prospective buyers what you've shown me—evidence of a leaky roof and signs of termites.

They decided to pass. And frankly, I'm glad. They're a sweet old couple and they don't want problems like that at their age. That house would suit younger folk who appreciate a bargain and are prepared to do a little work.''

Max shook his head. ''No wonder Ray was pissed at you. Isn't he aware of the Realtors' Code of Ethics?''

''He can cite chapter and verse. *He's* not a pest control expert, so how would he know there are termites? Nor is he a builder. Therefore he can't advise anyone about the roof, as it's out of his area of expertise. I told him, 'How can I sell houses I know have problems and not say anything? If those people moved in they would practically be my neighbors.'''

''Did you ever stop to think maybe you're in the wrong business?'' Max asked mildly.

Kelly heard an old rebuke. ''Don't say it.''

''What?''

''What you're thinking—that I should quit my job.'' She picked up his glass to take a sip and discovered bourbon mixed with the Coke. *Strange.* Max wasn't a drinker; the bourbon usually only came out when they had company. ''Is something wrong, Max?''

An odd flicker of alarm crossed his face as he took

the glass from her hand and drained it. "Nothing's wrong."

Kelly felt his forehead with the back of her hand. "Are you sure? You don't seem yourself tonight."

"Yeah, sure," he muttered. "I'm fine."

Kelly searched his averted profile a moment more, then shrugged, took up a spoon and tasted the chili. "Needs salt."

Max batted her hand away. "*I'm* doing the cooking."

Robyn, their eldest daughter at twelve years of age, hurried into the room. She was dressed in her leotard, toe shoes dangling from her hand and her dark hair tied back in a knot. "Da-a-ad, I'm going to be late for ballet," she wailed, then stopped when she saw Kelly. "Where've *you* been?"

"Working. And don't use that tone with me. If you're ready to go, I'll take you. Have you had dinner?"

"No." Robyn found her running shoes in the pile of footwear by the back door and sat on a straight-back chair to lace them up.

"Max!" Kelly said. "You could at least have made sure she'd eaten."

Max's expression turned cold, causing Kelly's stomach to sink. Tonight, of all nights, she wished she hadn't sniped at him. These days, one wrong word, one reproach or testy comment from either side, was all it took to set them off.

"Robyn's old enough to get herself something to eat," Max informed her. "And I've got other things to do besides fix dinner and chauffeur the kids around."

"You didn't *have* to make dinner tonight."

"If you weren't so wrapped up in yourself these days, Kelly, you'd know I'm behind on *all* my projects, not just the Whidbey Island house. And the reason I'm behind is that I've had to pick up the slack for *you*."

If anything upset her it was the suggestion that she wasn't meeting her responsibilities. "Maybe *you're* taking on too much work. For thirteen years I've been a devoted wife and mother. Now that the twins don't need me as much, don't I deserve a career of my own?"

"I might not mind if I thought you enjoyed your job, but all you do is complain about Ray and then give in to his every demand on your time. What about me and the kids…when do you make time for *us*?"

"I do enjoy my job—"

"Stop it!" Robyn shrieked, and stomped over to the fridge. "I don't want dinner. I'll eat an apple on the way."

The volume on the TV had steadily climbed to compensate for their raised voices. Now Max yelled, "Beth! Turn that TV *down*."

Beth, her light brown hair tousled, peered over the back of the couch, anxiously scanning her parents. The volume dropped abruptly.

Max picked up a spice jar and with jerking movements shook half the bottle of chili powder into the pot.

"Oh, great!" Kelly said, throwing up her hands. "Now the twins won't eat it."

"What won't we eat?" Tina said, running into the room, with Tammy close on her heels, their identical blond curls bouncing midway down their backs. Billy and Flora swirled around their legs. The preschoolers stopped short at the sight of Max's scowling face and, with identical wide blue eyes, glanced uneasily at their mother.

"Hi, girls. Did you have a good day?" Kelly stooped to gather her little ones into her arms, eager to maintain a semblance of peace for the children's sake. How quickly these angry exchanges between her and Max could flare up scared her.

"We made finger puppets in play school," Tina said, holding up a cardboard cylinder decorated with colored pieces of felt. "I'm Tweedledee."

"And I'm Tweedledum." Tammy waggled her puppet close to Kelly's face.

"Lovely. You can put on a play for us after dinner."

The twins squirmed out of her arms and ran off to crouch beneath the breakfast bar so they could dance their puppets above the edge for their father's benefit. The dogs trotted off to the kitchen, sniffing the floor for fallen scraps.

Kelly swallowed past the lump in her throat and walked over to the family room to flick on a floor lamp, then drew the blinds against the encroaching darkness. "Hi, Beth. How did your spelling test go?"

"I got forty-eight out of fifty," said the ten-year-old without taking her eyes off the preteen adventure show playing out on the TV.

"That's wonderful, honey. Aren't you glad we went over your list of words that one last time?"

"Mom, I'm ready," Robyn called. "Can we leave?"

Kelly was following her daughter out the front door, when Max appeared in the hallway. "Are you coming back?"

She stared at him. "Of course. Why wouldn't I?"

"You might stop off at the office, for all I know."

"Well, I'm not going to." She reached for his hand. "Max, please. Let's not fight."

He squeezed her hand, then dropped it, suddenly looking very tired. "The last thing I want is to fight."

Kelly drove Robyn to ballet in silence, her mind circling around her argument with Max. Ever since she'd started working, their relationship had been rocky. So what if she refused to give up her job or hire a housekeeper? She was coping. If he was fair he'd admit that not only *her* job caused problems. His business was expanding and the demands of work and family often overwhelmed them both.

Robyn's worried voice broke into her thoughts. "Are you and Daddy going to get divorced?"

Kelly's hands jerked on the wheel, making the car swerve across the center line. "Where did you get that idea?"

"You're always fighting." Robyn's face looked pale in the dim light between street lamps. "Janie's mother and father were like that before they split up."

"Yes, but..." Kelly sputtered, still taken aback that Robyn had even brought the subject up. "That's *them*. Your father and I...we're different."

"How?"

"We love each other."

"Do you?"

Kelly stared straight ahead. *Did* they still love each other? Or was it a fiction they were desperately trying to maintain? They'd been high-school sweethearts; if they met today for the first time, would they have anything in common?

"Yes," she said firmly, to convince herself as much as her daughter. "We love each other. And we're *not* getting divorced."

She pulled to a halt in front of the ballet school and turned to touch Robyn's cheek. "Your father and I have some problems, but they're work related. There's nothing big enough or bad enough to stop us from being a family. Don't worry, honey. Okay? I'll see you in an hour."

Robyn shook her head. "Janie's mom's picking us up and I'm staying overnight. Dad said it was okay."

"All right, then. See you tomorrow."

When she got home, the TV was off and Max was reading to the twins from their favorite Richard Scarry book. Beth was probably in her room, playing her Game Boy. Kelly glanced at the uncleared dining table and the two bowls of uneaten chili con carne and shook her head.

Were she and Max still going out? She wasn't

even sure she wanted to any longer. Tension had tied her stomach in knots and ruined her appetite.

''I'm going out to the plant room,'' she said to no one in particular. Time spent with her dried flowers always soothed her nerves.

The plant room was an addition to the already sprawling outbuilding Max had built in the northeast corner of the property. The main shed housed the gardening equipment and barbecue. To that, Max had added a chicken coop with nesting space for three chickens, and finally a long narrow section in which Kelly dried flowers and worked on her floral arrangements.

She pushed through the door, comforted by its familiar creak, and was enveloped by the mingled scents of drying flowers. French lavender, roses, Sweet Annie, strawflowers, yarrow, baby's breath, blue larkspur, Marguerite daisies and more, hung in bunches from overhead wires strung the length of the room.

She'd settled onto a high stool at the bench and was working on an arrangement of barley, oats and red rosebuds to the comfortable sound of hens clucking as they roosted for the night, when she heard a knock. The door opened and Max came in. Kelly's hands stilled on pale gold stalks, as she tensed for another argument.

His outstretched hand held a glass of wine. "I thought maybe you could use this."

"Thanks." She softened; this was his way of apologizing. "I'm sorry about earlier."

Max came closer, cupped her face in his hands and kissed her until her knees felt as soft and warm as soap melting in hot water. Kelly's spirits lifted. They hadn't made love in weeks. Or was it months? She'd lost track as their sex life had gone from fireworks to fizzle, but this weekend could still turn out to be special.

"Your anniversary present is in my briefcase," she told him when at last he drew back. "I'll go get it."

"Stay here," Max said. "I'll do it."

He returned a few minutes later, bearing a square yellow envelope inscribed with his name. Anxiously, Kelly watched him open it. He was always saying she should be less practical and more romantic, but was this going too far? She hadn't had a lot of time to consider the matter.

Max pulled out the card and a gift voucher fell out. His first reaction, quickly covered, was one of dismay. "Latin-dance lessons?"

"Okay, so it's really for both of us. But it'll be fun, I promise you. And it's something we can do together." She smiled slyly. "Tango, the salsa, the lambada... Latin dancing is *very* sexy."

"Sexy? Maybe we could use a little...ahem, *exercise*. Thanks, Kel." He tucked the card back in the envelope. "I'm afraid you're going to have to wait awhile for your present."

In other words, he hadn't gotten around to buying her anything. Kelly hid her disappointment. He'd given her those beautiful roses, after all. "That's okay."

He kissed her again. "Are you going to be long? Nancy's here."

"I'll be right out. Where shall we go for dinner?"

Casually he brushed a finger over the silky fringe of an oat head. "I hope you're not too hungry...."

"I'm *starving*. Don't tell me you ate with the kids."

"No, no. But maybe you'd better have a snack before we go. It'll take a couple of hours to get to the restaurant."

"A couple of hours? *Where* are you taking me?"

A grin widened his angular jaw, his first full-on smile of the evening. "I made reservations for the Salish Lodge at Snoqualmie Falls. We drive up tonight for the weekend. Kind of like a second honeymoon. That's my present to you. To us.''

"Oh, Max! That is fantastic." She rose and threw her arms around his neck. "I love you!"

Max lifted Kelly right off the ground and held her tightly against him. "Don't ever stop loving me, Kel," he whispered against her neck. "I couldn't bear it."

CHAPTER TWO

MAX OFTEN SURPRISED HER with a romantic gesture, but a weekend at the Salish Lodge was positively inspired. The roaring wood fire with its scent of burning pine, the warmth and elegance of the rustic furniture, and the hot tub for two…all promised a weekend of cozy intimacy.

Kelly accepted the crystal flute Max handed her. "Heavenly. But can we afford Dom Pérignon?"

"Sometimes you just have to say to hell with the cost, Kel." He shifted closer to her on the love seat and held her gaze. "To us. Whoever said thirteen was an unlucky number was wrong."

Clinking glasses, Kelly repeated, "To us. And to another thirteen years." Thirteen had better *not* be unlucky; they needed all the help they could get.

Max sipped his champagne and set the glass on the coffee table. "Did I tell you I sent off my entry for the Stonington Award today?"

"Really? Which house? What category?"

"The split level in Falkner's Cove. Luxury domicile. If I win—heck, even if I get nominated—my career should take off. I'd finally be able to keep you in the style to which you'd like to become accustomed.''

''I always knew you'd make it.''

''With a boost to our income, we could hire a cleaner,'' Max said. ''Stop you from spreading yourself too thin.''

''I can manage. I always have.'' Hiring a cleaner would mean she wasn't doing her job at home, and Kelly took pride in being a good mother *and* housekeeper. ''There's no reason I can't do it all.''

''Come on, Kel. We've had this argument before.''

''Too many times,'' she agreed. ''Let's drop it for now.'' She took Max's sigh for acquiescence and snuggled up to him, enjoying the weight of his arm draped around her shoulder. ''This is just like our first honeymoon.''

''Not quite,'' Max murmured, nibbling her ear. ''The first time we came here we were in bed before we could unpack.''

She glanced over her shoulder at the king-size bed and back at Max. ''Down your bubbly, soldier. We're going in.''

Kelly stripped off her clothes, recalling how, on their first honeymoon, Max had removed them for her. Thirteen years on, lovemaking wasn't the mad, passionate event it once was, and a long time had passed since they'd gone to bed with the express purpose of having sex. Nowadays they mostly fell asleep right away, exhausted by a full day of work, chores and responsibilities.

But whether it was the champagne or the romantic setting or the promise of a weekend to themselves, once beneath the down comforter, with her bare breasts pressed to Max's chest, Kelly forgot everything except the heat moving through her veins and the gladness in her heart that they were here, making love, instead of warring at home.

She trailed kisses beneath his jaw, testing the texture of his skin with her tongue. "Mmm, you taste good. You did remember to bring condoms, didn't you?"

"Uh-huh." His hands slid down her back and over her hips, bringing her closer. "But do we have to use them?"

"Until I get fitted with another IUD, yes. Dr. Johnson said my body should have a short rest from the device."

Max nudged a knee between hers. "It's been a while since we've made love. You feel really good, Kel."

"Go get the condoms, Max, before we get carried away."

With a sigh, he pulled back, but only to take her face in his hands. "When are we going to have another baby? After the twins, you agreed we'd have more."

She twisted away from his searching gaze. "I don't recall—"

"Yes, you did. When you took the job with Ray you said, 'It's something to do until we have another child.' That was over a year and a half ago. When, Kelly? When are we going to have another kid?"

"I don't know. Someday. When the time is right."

"The twins start school next year, which'll leave you free to care for a new baby."

"Or to pursue my career." She rolled over, shutting him out. "Don't pressure me, Max. I have so little that's all my own."

"You have your flowers."

She snorted derisively. "Dried-flower arrangements I give away to friends—it's a hobby. I want to contribute to the household, too."

"You do, immeasurably. Not all contributions are monetary. And money isn't necessarily the most important contribution."

"Try running a household without it. If you think I spread myself too thin now, what would I be like with another baby?'' He had no answer to that. Kelly felt bad at disappointing him. Now she vaguely remembered she *had* agreed to have more children. But that had been before she knew how important having a job of her own would become to her. ''I'm sorry, Max. I know you want a son.''

His silence took on a strained quality. She turned back to him, shocked to see his face drained of color. ''Good grief, Max, you're as white as the sheets.''

''I love the girls, Kel,'' he said earnestly.

''Of course you do.'' He was so sweet, so silly, sometimes. ''Go get the condoms.''

He left her and went to his suitcase. A moment later she heard him swear. ''What is it?''

He turned to her, his open hands empty. ''I bought a new box especially for this weekend. I was positive I put it in my suitcase. Now I can't find it.''

Oh, great. Their big romantic weekend and they couldn't make love. She glanced at the bedside digital clock. By now it was so late the hotel store would surely be shut. Max looked so disappointed and frustrated she beckoned him with a smile. ''Never mind. I'm sure one night won't hurt. Come here, lover.''

MAX AWOKE EARLY, A LITTLE tired but with a lingering sense of deep satisfaction. The night before they'd made love not once but twice—something they hadn't done in years, not since before the twins were born.

Kelly slept on, one hand tucked under her chin. She was so familiar to him that sometimes he couldn't *see* her. Mentally he traced the lines of her face, the short straight nose, the cheekbones she wished were higher, the sweetly curving mouth and small chin. Out of context, she became a stranger again. A pretty, sexy stranger.

He skimmed a finger down the bridge of her nose, and she reached up in her sleep to scratch. He waited until her hand fell away, then did it again.

Her eyes, deep brown in the half light, opened. When she saw him watching her, two small vertical lines pulled her eyebrows together. "Don't wake me up," she mumbled sleepily. "You know I hate being woken up."

The pretty sexy stranger would have wanted him to wake her up. Max sighed and slid out of bed to head for the shower.

As the steaming water sluiced over him, he considered Randall. He had to tell Kelly about the boy, and he would, but not until they'd had more time to cement their closeness. Another day should be enough. A hike in the woods, a nice dinner, a Jacuzzi in the evening, followed by more lovemaking…

When he came out of the bathroom, a towel

wrapped around his waist, Kelly was sitting up in bed, combing her fingers through her hair.

"Come here," she said, fully awake now and smiling.

Max leaned in for a kiss. Instead of meeting his lips, Kelly rubbed her cheek over his freshly shaven jaw. "I love it when you're all smooth and yummy smelling. Come back to bed." She tried to pull him down on top of her.

"Later." He yanked the covers off the bed, making her giggle and shriek. "Get up, woman. We've got ground to cover."

Ravenous after the previous night, they ate enormous plates of bacon and eggs in the hotel dining room, then set off on the trail that zigzagged down the cliff beside the river. Through the trees, they could hear the roar of Snoqualmie Falls.

"I wonder how the kids are doing?" Kelly said. "I hope Nancy made them breakfast and didn't just let them snack on junk."

Max stopped abruptly. "We need to make a rule for this weekend—no talking about the kids or our jobs."

"But—" Kelly began, then said "—you're right. No kids. No jobs."

Twenty minutes later the silence stretched. "What are you thinking?" Max finally asked.

"I'm thinking I should have done a load of laundry before we left so Beth's judo outfit would be clean for her training session Monday."

"No kids, no jobs, no *chores*."

"But, Max, that's our life," Kelly protested, only half joking.

"Look at that." He paused at the observation deck, with its view of the falls—a foaming spill of white water dropping nearly three hundred feet down the cliff face. "It's more spectacular than I remembered." Max took in a deep breath that made his chest rise beneath his plaid flannel shirt. "This is wonderful. Fresh air, exercise, good food, great sex..." He pulled Kelly close and breathed in the scent of her hair. "And my best gal by my side."

She slipped her arms around his waist. "Your *only* gal, don't you mean?"

He kissed her forehead and the tip of her nose and would have continued on down to her mouth.

"Max," Kelly began, interrupting him. "Did you mean what you said last night about not wanting a boy?"

Her speculative tone and searching gaze put him immediately on guard. He'd reacted too strongly to her innocent suggestion that he wanted a son. She'd take it as a sign he was hiding something. As he was. "Why wouldn't I mean it?"

"I've always wondered," she went on, undeterred by his feeble protest, "if you weren't a teeny bit disappointed we had all girls."

He wanted to reassure her that wasn't the case; hell, he wished he could convince *himself.* But the words stuck in his throat. The letter from Randall had brought his emotions too close to the surface for him to be able to lie.

Avoiding eye contact, he muttered something unintelligible and returned to the path that led to the river.

"Max!" Kelly hurried after him, sending twigs and small stones skittering. "What's wrong with you?"

"Nothing."

"I asked you something important, and instead of answering, you stride off without a word. I want to know what's wrong."

"There's nothing wrong. Just forget it."

"You *never* talk about your feelings," Kelly complained. "This weekend is an opportunity to work out some of the kinks in our relationship. You can't just walk away from an emotionally difficult subject."

"Feelings. You always want to talk about feelings."

He strode on. Talking about that stuff made him

uncomfortable; it highlighted what was *wrong* with their relationship, instead of focusing on what was *right*. And whenever Kelly started discussing their problems, he felt he'd failed her somehow. Not that he would ever admit it.

She called again, exasperated. "Max!"

"If you would quit working or cut back your hours," he yelled over his shoulder, "we might not *have* kinks in our relationship."

Throwing a blatant red herring in her path was a dirty trick, but he hadn't yet figured out what he was going to do about Randall, and until he did, he didn't want to talk about sons, real or hypothetical.

"That is so unfair!" She kicked her booted foot at a rotting stump beside the path, scattering crumbling bits of decaying wood.

He shrugged and kept on walking. "You wanted to know what I thought."

"You're avoiding the real issue," she insisted. "You want another child and I…I'm not ready."

He snapped a dry twig off a branch in passing and flung it down the hillside, where it snagged on a bush. "You keep saying 'maybe' and 'later,' but later never comes and maybe means nothing. Face it, you have no intention of having another baby."

"I never said that!"

"You didn't have to." Fed up, he increased his pace.

Max felt her angry silence bombard his back as they descended toward the valley floor around hairpin turns in the narrow path. Gradually his temper cooled. He could put their spat from his mind, if not the cause of it, but he knew Kelly would continue to dwell on the problem until they made up.

With a sigh, he stopped again, took her in his arms and rubbed her nose with his. "I forgive you."

She snorted, half amused, half annoyed, but wholly unrelenting. "Max, you *know* we should talk more."

"Aw, Kel, it's too nice a day to hash things over. Come on, we're almost at the river."

Reluctantly she gave up the fight. "Oh, all right."

Another hundred feet and the trail led them out of the woods to the edge of the tumbling river. Silenced by the roar of water and awed by the grandeur of the falls, they turned to each other. His hands lightly touching her waist, he kissed her, putting all the tenderness he could into the soft pressure on her lips, and he felt her irritation dissolve in the misty air.

High overhead, treetops were moving in the wind, which blew clouds across the sun, but there on the river all was still and warm. They walked along the gorge until they came to a large flat rock where they could sit side by side, looking toward the falls.

From her day pack Kelly removed the lunch the hotel had prepared for them. "Want a sandwich?" she asked, speaking over the sound of water. He nodded and she handed him one. "Remember when we came here on our honeymoon? We smuggled our own food into the hotel because we didn't have the money to buy meals."

"How did you get stuck with such a cheap bastard?"

"I guess I got lucky," Kelly said, munching happily.

"Do you still think you're lucky?" Max tossed a breadcrumb to a junco that had fluttered down onto the next rock. The small gray bird snapped up the crumb in its beak and turned its black head to regard him with one beady eye. Kelly still hadn't answered. "Never mind," Max said. "Dumb question."

"We were so young when we married," she said at last. "I was straight out of high school and you were only a year older." Kelly placed a hand on his jaw, forcing him to look at her. "I can't imagine life without you." She shook her head with a wry grin. "Sometimes I can't imagine life *with* you, either."

He nudged her off balance, then caught her before she toppled. She fell into his arms, laughing. He said,

"I'll never understand why your grandmother allowed you to marry so young. If you'd been *my* daughter..."

"She let Geena go to New York on a modeling contract when she was sixteen. How could she stop me from marrying at eighteen? Gran always told us we had good heads on our shoulders and that we should trust our own judgment."

"Bulldust. You and your sisters were as headstrong as wild ponies. You always got your way. Erin was the most sensible, but your Gran was as weak as water where you girls were concerned."

"Don't you criticize Gran," she said, wagging a finger at him. "At least she considered my feelings. Your parents did everything they could to stop us from getting engaged. The moment they heard we wanted to get married after graduation they shipped you off to that job on the dude ranch, hoping you'd forget me over the summer."

The bite of sandwich in his mouth suddenly turned dry and lumpy. Why the hell had he brought up the past? "But I didn't, did I?" he demanded, feeling an urgent need to reconnect with Kelly. He did not want to lose the woman he'd spent more than a decade building a life with.

She tilted her head, clearly puzzled by his tone.

"No," she said slowly. "You came home even more loving than when you left…if that's possible."

He kissed her, almost desperately, deepening the kiss until she melted against him, as he'd hoped she would, and slid her arms around his neck.

Finally she drew back, eyes grave. "All right, Max. You'd better tell me all about it."

Despite the warm sun, a chill raised bumps on Max's forearms. How could she know? He'd hidden the letter from Randall deep in the bottom drawer of his office filing cabinet. "What do you mean?"

"You're hiding something," Kelly stated. "You've been acting really weird all weekend, guilty and secretive—when you weren't giving me a tumble, that is." She crossed her arms. "Spill it."

At first Kelly thought he would evade this demand for explanations, too. Then before her eyes, Max seemed to shrink from her and turn inward. Her heart sank. Whatever he was hiding must be really bad. He was having an affair. He wanted a divorce. He—

"I have a son."

She stared. She'd heard him speak, but his words had no meaning. "What did you say?"

"I have a son," he repeated.

"That's impossible. Unless," she added with a short humorless laugh, "one of the twins had a sex change."

"Kelly."

"But it's impossible, Max," she repeated. "We were married right out of high school. How could you have a child I don't know about?"

"I got a letter from him yesterday." Max crumpled the plastic wrap his sandwich had come in and compressed it into a tiny ball. "His name is Randall Tipton. He's thirteen years old and he lives in Wyoming."

The bottom fell out of Kelly's world. One moment the sun was shining on her and Max, a *unit* despite their problems, as solid as the rock on which they were sitting. The next instant she was in free fall, with no hope of safe landing.

Questions crowded her tongue, clamoring for expression. "But how…? When…? *Who is the mother?*"

"Her name is Lanni. She worked at the dude ranch."

Spinning, sinking, Kelly spiraled down through a swirling gray void. *"You had an affair with another woman while you were engaged to me?"*

"You'd broken off the engagement before I left for the ranch, remember?"

"Your *parents* broke it off. I had every intention of marrying you as soon as we had the opportunity. I thought you felt the same."

He stared at her as if she were speaking a foreign language. "You said we should go along with their wishes. I left for Wyoming thinking you weren't going to marry me."

"I thought you'd come sweeping back one moonlit night and carry me away, that we would elope or something equally romantic. Instead…" Tears swam in her eyes as she gazed at him, stricken, "You were with this Lanni person."

He tried to take her hand. "Forget Lanni. She's not important."

"How can you say she's not important?" Kelly shrilled, tugging away. "She's the mother of your child."

Kelly wrapped her arms around her shivering body and buried her face in her knees. Max, her anchor, her *rock,* the husband she thought she knew inside out, had suddenly, nightmarishly, become a stranger.

"Dear God, Max," she said in a broken whisper. "What have you done to us?"

He was silent.

"Did you know before you got the letter you had a child?"

"Yes. Although until yesterday I didn't know he was a boy."

"And that made the difference. That's why you're telling me now," she said, struggling to understand.

"No. It's the letter."

Her stomach heaved; she gripped herself tighter. "All these years *you knew you had a child and you never told me.*"

"I wanted to put it all behind me."

Suddenly she was furious. She sprang to her feet on the rock. "What gives you the right to put a child behind you? To walk away and forget it ever existed?"

"Do you think that was easy for me?" he cried. "Do you think I haven't wondered and worried all these years whether or not he or she was growing up happy and healthy?"

"How would I know?" she shouted. "You didn't tell me!"

Her voice echoed off the cliff face, startling her into awareness of their surroundings. She took a deep breath, then another. "Okay, let's calm down." She sat again, forcing herself to ignore the pain that was eating away at her like acid. "You'd better start at the beginning and explain."

Max told her the whole story. The dude ranch, Lanni pursuing him, the pregnancy, the subsequent meetings between both sets of parents. Kelly noticed he glossed over the part where he'd capitulated to Lanni's advances. Fine, she sure didn't want to hear about that, although it had always been her experience that it took two to tango.

"Lanni's family were strong Catholics. They wouldn't hear of abortion," Max went on. "My parents gave her money to pay for medical expenses and kept in touch with her parents throughout the pregnancy. The baby was put up for adoption and…" He gazed at his hands, twisted together. "That was the last I'd heard of the child. Like I said, until yesterday I didn't even know if it was a boy or a girl."

At the ache in his voice part of her, amazingly, wanted to comfort him for the years of loss. He was a loving and responsible father and she knew he must feel guilt and regret.

An instant later, her heart hardened. Had he considered *her* feelings when he'd slipped away from the bunkhouse at midnight for a rendezvous with Lanni?

A chilly raindrop hit her cheek and she glanced up to see the sun had completely disappeared behind the gray clouds massing around the mountain peaks. "It's starting to rain. We'd better head back."

The rain came on with sudden violence, in driving sheets that turned the dirt trail to mud and the bushes and trees to dripping greenery that slid from their grasp as they pulled themselves up the slippery track. By the time they'd arrived back at the lodge, they were soaked through and cloaked in mud from the knees down.

In their room Kelly began to haphazardly pile sweaters and underwear into her suitcase, not even bothering to change out of her wet clothes.

"What are you doing?" Max demanded, toweling his head. His pale hair had turned dark with rain and now stuck out in spikes. "We're booked for another night."

"I can't sleep in this bed with you." She tossed in her cosmetics case with an angry jerk of her wrist. "Not with your affair making a mockery of last night and of every night of our marriage. I want to be with my children."

"Kelly, for God's sake." He threw down the towel and tried to take her in his arms. "Don't do this."

Shrugging him off, she snapped the locks shut on her suitcase and faced him, chin in the air. "I want to go home."

On the drive back to Hainesville, Kelly couldn't look at Max. In her mind, she replayed endlessly that summer they were apart. How could she not have known he was up to no good? How could she not have gleaned from his infrequent phone calls and hesitant assurances of affection that he had someone else on a string? At the time she'd put his awkwardness down to the difficulty of communicating on the public telephone in the lodge. God, but she'd been naive.

Max slid his hand onto her knee and squeezed tentatively. "Talk to me, Kelly."

"I have nothing to say." Her voice was as dead as love gone wrong.

"Come on, you must. What are you feeling?"

"What am I *feeling?*" She twisted in her seat to face him. "*Now* you want to talk. Suddenly you're interested in *feelings*. Well, listen up. I'm *hurting,* Max. I never imagined I could hurt this badly. And I'm *angry*. I'm so furious I could kill you. While *I* was sewing my wedding dress, *you* were sleeping with another woman. While *I* was counting the days until we could start a family, *you* were making a baby without me. While *I* poured out my heart in long loving letters, *you* were already lying to me. Our whole marriage is a lie."

"Kelly, you know that's not true."

Scalding tears heated her already flushed cheeks. "You led me to believe I was your first, just as you were my first. And only. How many other women have you had that you haven't told me about?"

"None."

"How can I believe you?"

He didn't answer. Finally, in a low voice, he said, "I guess you can't. You have to trust me."

With a snort, she threw up her hands. "Trust? What's that?"

"Except for that one time, I've never lied to you or cheated on you."

Kelly rubbed her hands over her face, suddenly exhausted, as though her anger had drained all the energy out of her. "I know. Or do I? That's the problem. I'll never know for sure."

Silenced, Max drove on through the rain and the dark. Once or twice she glanced sideways, to see his hands gripping the wheel and his jaw set. He was thinking about Randall. She couldn't stop thinking about the boy, either.

She didn't *want* to talk, but she *had* to.

Her fury had dissipated, leaving behind an icy calmness that frightened her almost as much. "I can't believe you fathered a baby and didn't tell me."

He took his gaze off the road. "I was eighteen. I was stupid. And too much in love with you to risk losing you by confessing the truth."

"And now you're not."

The blaring horn of a passing semitrailer snapped his attention back to the wet highway. "Not what?"

"In love with me," she said, exasperated by his inability to grasp the logic. "Now you can tell the truth because you don't love me anymore and don't care if you lose me.''

''For God's sake, Kelly. That's not true. It's only come up because the boy contacted me.''

He had a son, not by her. Calmness deserted her as hysteria clawed at her throat. ''The boy, the boy. He's the *boy* you always wanted.''

''You know I love the girls more than anything. Randall isn't going to change that.''

''You're already saying his name as if you know him. What does he want, anyway?''

Max shrugged. ''Just to see me. He's curious about his biological parents. And no, I don't know if he's contacted Lanni.''

''Do…do you want to meet him?''

''Yes. Would that bother you?''

She stared at him. ''Are you crazy? It would tear me apart. It would tear *us* apart.''

Max shook his head. ''You're overreacting.''

''Don't tell me I'm overreacting,'' she warned. ''You don't know how I feel. What are the girls going to think?''

''They might be pleased to have a big brother.''

Kelly refused to even contemplate that scenario. ''You went straight from me to her.''

''No, not right away. It was—''

''Please, I don't want details.'' She stared out the

window, watching the dark sodden shapes of trees flicker past. "How long?"

"Three weeks." She winced, and he reminded her, "*You* called off our engagement."

"You could at least say you're sorry."

"I never meant to hurt you, Kelly. What is the real issue? Is it that I slept with another woman, or the fact that I had a child you didn't know about?"

In the reflection from the window, Kelly watched raindrops stream down her face. Lanni, the lies by omission, the secret he'd kept from her all these years. Hurt didn't begin to describe how she felt, and forgiveness wasn't even on the horizon.

"I can't separate the two."

What she couldn't say, even to Max, was how inadequate she felt at never having given him a son. Max didn't value her work outside the home; he only valued her as the mother of his children. She hadn't even gotten that right. Supposedly the man's sperm determined whether a child was a boy or a girl, but he'd had a boy with another woman. Maybe it was Kelly's own body chemistry that had favored the survival of a sperm with an X chromosome and caused her to produce nothing but girls.

She had a bad feeling in her gut about Randall, and she didn't think it was just because she was jealous of Lanni. Her and Max's marriage had been on shaky ground for more than a year. If Max let this boy into their lives, he would turn them all upside down. He might somehow take Max away from her and the girls.

They got home late; the kids were in bed and Nancy was watching TV in the family room. Hiding her tear-stained face from the surprised teenager, Kelly went straight to the bedroom while Max made up some excuse for their early return. She heard the front door shut, and a few minutes later Max came into the room. He had a piece of folded foolscap in his hand. The letter.

"Would you like to read it?" he asked.

"No."

He held out a photograph and tried to show her. "He looks like a nice kid."

"I don't want to see." She pushed him away, then grabbed his arm. "Oh, give it here."

Thoughts of DNA testing to prove paternity dissolved as she gazed at a younger version of Max. Randall's eyes, the angle of his jaw, the slight tilt of his head were all pure Max, even if the boy's coloring was not. Kelly's head began to throb. She hadn't wanted the kid to be real to her and now he was. "Let me see the letter."

Reading Randall's words compounded her mistake. She felt a physical ache in her heart from empathizing with the boy. *No,* she thought, deliberately shutting down her feelings. She could never feel anything warmer than dislike for Max's son by another woman.

"He's got a good home, with loving adoptive parents," she said callously, thrusting the letter aside. "He doesn't need you."

"Maybe not," Max agreed tightly. "Maybe I need him."

Kelly closed her eyes on a sharp stab of pain, unable to speak.

"He wants to meet me," Max went on. "I'd like to meet him, too."

Opening her eyes, she reached for his arm. "Don't go, Max," she pleaded. "For the girls' sake if not for mine. You can't undo the past, but to some extent you can choose your future."

"I want to meet him," he repeated. "Kelly, he's my *son.*"

"I…I'm not sure I can go on living with you if you contact that boy." She knew she sounded melodramatic, but she was desperate.

"I can't live with my conscience if I *don't* contact him." Max slipped the photo back into the envelope and spoke with a new determination. "Randall's part of me, Kel. You can't just ignore him, and I won't. I'm going to Wyoming. I'm going to see my son."

CHAPTER THREE

MAX'S LAST THOUGHT before his finger touched the doorbell of Randall's house in Jackson two weeks later was, *Am I doing the right thing?* Then the chimes sounded, and whether or not coming here against Kelly's wishes was right, the point became moot. He could hardly run away, or pretend to be a door-to-door salesman. Besides, now that he knew of Randall's existence, nothing would stop him from meeting his son.

Yet he wondered at the wheelchair ramp that paralleled the steps to the front door. The photo of Randall had been head and shoulders only. Could he be handicapped?

Max heard footsteps inside the house and wiped his palms against his slacks; he hadn't expected to feel so nervous. Would the boy like him? Would he blame him for the past? Could Max bear to find a son and not keep him? Would Kelly forgive him if he did?

The door opened. The boy in the photograph,

standing firmly on two feet, stared back at him through clunky glasses. His pressed cotton shirt was buttoned up to the collar and his gabardine pants held a perfect crease. Randall turned a fiery red that clashed with his carroty hair and stammered a greeting. "H-hello. Are you...?"

"I'm Max. Hi, Randall." Max reached for his son's hand. The contact almost undid him; suddenly his throat was thick and his eyes moist. He coughed, Randall shuffled his feet, and their hands fell apart.

"Come in and meet my parents," Randall said. "They're in the living room."

Randall's parents had insisted on meeting him, and Max couldn't blame them—for all they knew, he could be an ax murderer or a pedophile. But he hoped he and Randall would have some time alone; they'd need it if they were going to get past this awkward phase. *Patience.* He'd waited thirteen years for a son; he could wait a little longer.

He followed Randall into a room furnished with spare Scandinavian designs and a wall of books. A telescope on a tripod stood before a picture window looking across the broad valley known as Jackson Hole to the Grand Teton mountains. A baby grand piano dominated one corner, while precisely executed oil paintings of mountains and lakes lined the walls. The atmosphere was one of intellect and good taste, but to Max, used to the controlled chaos of life with four young children, the room seemed strangely sterile.

Mr. Tipton, dressed in a maroon cardigan and tie, rose as they entered and ran a hand sideways over his thinning pate, smoothing the sparse gray hairs into place. "Hello. I'm Marcus Tipton. This is my wife, Audrey."

"Nice to meet you both," Max said, extending his hand. "Are you the artist?" he asked Audrey, gesturing to the paintings.

"Clever of you to guess." Audrey smiled warmly up at Max from her wheelchair. She had on black slacks and an ivory twin set, and wore her smooth gray hair in a chin-length bob. "I'll get coffee. How do you take it, Mr. Walker?"

"Please, call me Max. Cream, no sugar. Thanks."

Max settled onto the couch catercorner to the chair in which Randall sat, hands folded on his knees, and let his mind run over his first impressions. Audrey was in a wheelchair, and Marcus Tipton had to be well over fifty; how did they keep up with an active teenage boy? Although judging from Randall's quiet demeanor that might not be a problem. No unrestrained bursts of youthful energy here.

Obviously, they'd managed perfectly well. Max was surprised and not very happy with his critical assumptions, and his protectiveness of a boy he hadn't raised. He had no rights here, he reminded himself, only privileges.

"Did you have a good flight?" Randall inquired politely. The question had the air of being rehearsed.

"Fine, thank you. I had a window seat and got a good view of Jackson as we landed. I'd forgotten how beautiful the country is around here."

Silence followed, awkward and begging to be filled. "Do you play any sports, Randall?"

"I played soccer when I was nine, but it was pretty wet and muddy and…" He glanced at his father, then at his hands. "I just didn't care for it."

"I see." Meaning he didn't see at all.

"Randall is more interested in intellectual pursuits," Marcus interjected. "Piano, the chess club, debating society, art…"

"Very commendable. You must be very proud of him."

Marcus smiled genially. "We are, indeed. He's never been anything but a credit to us. Top in his class, well respected by teachers and fellow students alike."

But did he have fun? Max wondered, then reproached himself for nitpicking. If any of his daughters achieved that kind of academic success he would be ecstatic.

He found himself looking for similarities between him and Randall. The boy had his build, tall and lean, and his long, tapered fingers. But Max's love of sport and his easy athleticism seemed to be missing from his son. Hell, he thought, the ability to sink a basketball wasn't exactly a genetic trait.

He turned to Marcus. "Do you have any other children?"

The older man shook his head. "Audrey and I weren't able to have children of our own. We planned to adopt more after Randall, but when Audrey lost the use of her legs in a car accident we decided against it."

"An accident," Max repeated. "Was Randall—" He broke off. Randall was *fine*. Even if he'd been in the car, he'd clearly survived intact.

"Randall was strapped into his booster seat in the back when the other car crossed the white line and hit the front of my wife's car. He had a few minor cuts, nothing serious."

"I'm sorry—about Audrey, that is. Dealing with the physical and emotional aftermath of a serious injury plus taking care of a toddler must not have been easy."

"We managed," Marcus said simply. "That's what you do when you're a family."

Max nodded. If there was an implied reproach he accepted it.

Marcus turned to Randall. "Son, could you help your mother with the tray, please?"

"Sure, Dad." Randall immediately got up and left the room.

Son. Dad. Max was reminded again that he was an outsider. No rights and only limited privileges.

Now that the boy was out of hearing, Marcus became serious. "We adopted Randall because we wanted to give a home to a baby whose parents couldn't care for him. Naturally, Audrey and I were concerned when after all these years he decided to contact his biological parents."

Max had a sudden sympathy for Marcus and Audrey; watching their son discover his biological father couldn't be easy for them.

"If my circumstances had been different when he was conceived…" Max spread his hands in the effort to explain. "I would have kept him. Maybe I should have tried harder to, but I couldn't—" He broke off. *Woulda, shoulda, coulda.* Pretty lame.

Marcus waved away Max's apologetic floundering. "All I meant was, Randall's been our whole life. For Audrey, especially. And Randall has been looking forward to meeting you so very much. His expectations are high and I'd hate to see him hurt. He's already been disappointed by his biological mother.''

"The last thing I want is for any of us to get hurt," Max said quietly. After a pause, he asked, ''What happened when he contacted Lanni?''

Marcus might have answered, but at that moment, Audrey wheeled into the room, followed by Randall bearing a tray laden with steaming cups and a plate of homemade banana bread. ''Coffee's ready.''

While Audrey served the cake, Randall handed around the coffee, impressing Max with his manners. Marcus and Audrey had done a good job with Randall on that score, at least.

''Would you like to see some of Randall's baby pictures?'' Audrey said to Max.

"I'd like that very much. Thank you.''

Flipping through early photos of Randall was an eerie experience. Aside from his hair coloring, he looked very much like Max had as a baby and he bore a family resemblance to all his daughters, especially Robyn. As he paged through Randall's first smile, first step, first day of school, Max couldn't help but be jealous of Marcus and Audrey for witnessing the milestones in his son's young life.

''He's obviously been raised in a loving home,'' Max said, handing the photo album back. ''I'm grateful…if that doesn't sound presumptuous.''

"Thank you," Audrey said. "It doesn't sound presumptuous at all." She glanced at her husband. "Well?"

Marcus nodded. "We'll leave you two now so you can get better acquainted."

Max watched them go, then turned to Randall. "They're nice people. They love you very much. And despite all that care and attention, they've managed to raise you unspoiled. You're lucky. *I'm* lucky."

Randall frowned. "Why are you lucky?"

Max smiled wryly. "That you've turned out so well lessens my guilt."

"I don't blame you for having me adopted out," Randall said earnestly. "I don't know why you gave me up, but you must have had good reasons."

"Your mother and I were too young to marry. Her parents wouldn't allow it." Not that he'd ever actually suggested it. To Max, that whole summer seemed like a bad dream. "Your father told me you contacted Lanni."

Randall's gaze dropped to the toes of his polished leather shoes. "She didn't want to meet me. She just got married last year and she's going to have a baby. She never told her husband about me and doesn't want to. She said I would make her life too complicated."

Max knew he shouldn't judge, but he could imagine Lanni saying something like that. His heart ached for the boy. "I'm sorry."

Randall shrugged. "Do you have other children?"

"My wife, Kelly, and I have four daughters."

"Four kids! Wow. I've always wished I had brothers and sisters. I mean, I wished I had a brother, but sisters would be okay—" He broke off, abashed. "Not that I expect you'd want me to meet them or anything."

Max shifted uncomfortably. "I would, but…to tell you the truth, Kelly wasn't too happy about me coming here."

"I'm sorry if I caused you trouble."

"Don't be." Max leaned over and squeezed Randall's forearm. "I wouldn't have missed this meeting for the world. I'm only sorry it didn't take place years ago."

"Did you…did you ever think of looking for me?"

The naked yearning in his voice dredged up a barge-load of guilt and regret in Max. The reasons he'd never gone looking for Randall had more to do with Kelly and Lanni than with the boy, but if he said that, wouldn't he be giving Randall the impression he wasn't important?

"I…I didn't want to disrupt your life."

''Oh. Okay.'' His dispassionate acceptance of the explanation made Max feel even worse. ''How old are your kids?''

''Robyn's twelve, Beth's ten and the twins, Tammy and Tina, are four years old.'' Max pulled out his wallet and extracted a photo. ''This was taken a year ago, but you get the idea.''

Randall studied the picture. ''You must have gotten married quite soon after…after you knew my biological mother.''

''Yes.''

''Were you in love with my mother?''

''I was very young. We were both very young. I don't think I knew what love was.'' Liar. He'd known then that he loved Kelly. But he had to give this kid *something*. ''Lanni was fun loving and adventurous. I liked her a lot.''

Randall handed back the photo. ''What do you do? I mean, for work?''

''I'm an architect. I design houses.''

''Wow. That's interesting. I like to draw. Sometimes I think I'd like to be an artist when I grow up. Would you like to see my sketchbook?''

Randall ran off to get his sketchbook and Max leaned against the couch and shut his eyes. He'd been naive to think Randall wouldn't want answers to difficult questions. Naive to think he could visit and go away again untouched. Randall was no longer just a face in a photograph or a product of his imagination. He was a boy with hopes and dreams, and Max himself was one of Randall's hopes and dreams. Marcus was right; Randall had expectations. The question was, could Max fulfill them?

And what were Max's expectations? He'd been so fired up to meet Randall, he hadn't thought through the consequences of an ongoing relationship, if there was to be one. He'd been focused on Kelly and overcoming her objections, instead of thinking about how he would incorporate a son into his life.

Randall returned and placed a well-used sketchbook in Max's lap. Max thumbed through meticulously executed pen-and-ink drawings of old barns, a mare and foal, a jackdaw on a pine branch. The boy had an eye for detail and a facility with his pen, although in Max's opinion the pictures were too careful to be really good. Like the drawings of a child afraid to color outside the lines, they lacked individuality.

"You show a great deal of promise," Max said, and Randall flushed beneath his freckles. "You're fortunate Audrey is interested in art. I'm sure she's very encouraging."

"She signed me up for art lessons when I was

ten,'' Randall said. "And she buys me any materials I want.''

"That's wonderful. What else do you like to do?''

"As Dad said, I play piano and chess and belong to the debating society. Oh, and I've recently built my own Web site so I can attract chess players from other countries.''

"What about friends? Do you hang out with a gang of kids from your school?''

"Not really,'' Randall admitted, pinching the crease in his pants. "I have a couple of friends in the chess club. But Mom gets migraines and can't handle having a bunch of noisy boys around. Not that I blame her,'' he said hastily. "Teenage boys can be very rowdy.''

Randall Tipton wouldn't know "rowdy" if he stepped in it, Max mused, then chastised himself for the uncharitable thoughts he was having toward Marcus and Audrey Tipton. They'd raised a well-behaved, polite young man who was a credit to his parents. And Randall seemed to be happy enough.

"Do you have a dog or a cat?'' Max asked.

"No, sir. Dad's allergic to pet fur. Actually, it's not the fur but the mites that live in the fur. I'm allowed to keep tropical fish, but they don't interact much with people. Do you have pets?''

Max almost didn't like to say. "Two dogs and some chickens."

A wistful gleam appeared in Randall's eyes. "My chess friend in Alaska has a husky. He scanned the dog's photo and e-mailed it to me."

"Well, Randall—" Max glanced at his watch "—I have to catch a plane back to Seattle in an hour. I'd better go." He'd deliberately ensured that his time here would be limited, just in case the meeting didn't work out. Now he wished he'd planned to stay the weekend. Maybe he and the boy could have gone horseback riding or fishing.

"I've enjoyed meeting you very much, sir," Randall said, rising.

"You don't have to call me sir."

"What should I call you, then?"

Max hesitated. He could hardly ask the boy to call him Dad; he already had a dad. "Max. Max will do just fine."

Randall walked him to the door. "Say goodbye to your folks for me," Max said, unwilling to share the final moments with his son with the Tiptons.

Randall stuck out his hand. Max took it, hesitated a second, then pulled the boy into a hug. The tightness in his chest seemed to expand until he found breathing difficult. "Take care."

They separated awkwardly, and Randall stared fixedly at his polished shoes. "W-will I see you again?"

Max had told himself this would be a one-off deal. More to the point, that was what he'd told Kelly. But how could he say no to his kid? Randall needed...*something* from him, some spark in his existence. And Max...well, Max needed to know that his son was okay. On the surface it certainly appeared that way. The boy had no material wants, he had parents who loved him and encouraged his interests, but Max sensed an underlying loneliness. He knew what it was to be an only child. "Lonely" was the one thing Max had never wanted for his children. It was the reason he'd had so many, and the reason he wanted still more.

Randall needed siblings. Max could give them to him.

"Would you like to visit my home and meet Kelly and your half sisters?" The words were out almost before he knew he was speaking, but he didn't regret them, not when he saw Randall's eyes light up.

"Oh, boy! Could I? When? I'll go ask Mom and Dad right now."

His heart telling him he'd done the right thing, Max followed his son back inside the house.

"YOU *WHAT!*" Kelly stared at Max. She was still coming to grips with the fact that he'd gone to Wyoming against her wishes.

Max sighed through gritted teeth and took the position that offense was the best form of defense. "I invited Randall to spend his summer vacation with us. Is that so hard to understand?"

"What's hard to understand is why you think I would agree," Kelly said, pacing the bedroom. "I told you I don't want anything to do with this kid."

Seated on the edge of the bed, Max followed her with his gaze. "I know I should have asked you first, but if you'd seen that boy you would have done the same thing. He lives with an elderly father and a wheelchair-bound mother. They're nice people and they're doing their best, but Randall has few friends. He's lonely. If he doesn't come to us he'll spend the summer in his room in front of the computer."

"My heart is breaking."

"Kelly, this sarcastic attitude isn't like you. If you only met him—"

"I don't want to meet him. What about me and the girls? Or don't you care about us anymore?" She stopped in front of the closet and took out her jacket.

"Of course I care. What are you doing?"

She ignored his question. "Having secret children and illicit love affairs isn't like the man I thought I married." Shrugging into her jacket, she stopped in front of him. "I thought I knew you. Now I realize I don't know you at all."

"Don't get sidetracked. We're talking about Randall. Please, Kel, give yourself time to get used to the idea."

"Are you serious? School gets out in a month. I'd need a lifetime to get used to this. Summer has always been family time."

"Randall *is* family, Kelly, whether you like it or not." He paused. "Where are you going?"

Kelly slipped her feet into a pair of loafers. "Gran's house."

"Can't we talk about this?"

"I'm too angry and upset to talk. I'll see you later. Maybe."

CHAPTER FOUR

WHEN KELLY GOT TO GRAN'S house she was surprised to see both her sisters' cars parked out front. She knocked once and let herself in the front door.

"Hello? Anybody home?" Lights burned in the living room to her left and she heard her sisters' voices.

"Is that you, Kel?" Erin, her eldest sister, called. "We're in here."

Kelly dropped her purse on the hall table and went through to the living room of the big Victorian house where Kelly and her sisters had grown up after her parents were killed in a car crash. Her younger sister, Geena, held her sleeping baby across her lap, and Erin's toddler was curled up in a portable cot Gran kept around for her great-grandchildren's frequent visits.

"You guys having a party without me...?" Kelly began, then stopped short at the sight of Gran, seated in her rocker with one leg propped up on a stool and an ice pack over her ankle.

"What happened?" Kelly demanded, hurrying across the room to her grandmother's side. "Are you all right, Gran?"

"Nothing serious. I just twisted my ankle while I was on my power walk this evening," Gran said, adjusting the ice pack.

"The ankle's badly swollen," Erin elaborated, pushing back her long blond hair. "I came by to drop off some homemade strawberry jam and found her crawling on her hands and knees."

"It's nothing," Gran insisted fretfully. "I'll be fine."

"I'm taking you to see Ben first thing in the morning," Geena said, referring to her husband, a local G.P. One hand rested lightly on little Sonja's rounded diaper-clad bottom. "I'd have brought him with me tonight, but he's doing an emergency appendectomy."

"You should have called me," Kelly scolded her Gran. She lifted the ice pack and winced at the swollen mottled skin. "Hang on and I'll get an Ace bandage from the first-aid kit in my car."

When she got back inside, Erin was administering anti-inflammatory tablets to the resistant septuagenarian. Kelly pulled up a stool before Gran's chair and expertly wrapped the elderly woman's ankle in a neat herringbone pattern.

"You're good, Kel," Geena said, admiring her sister's handiwork. "Where'd you learn to do that?"

"I take a refresher first-aid course every couple of years. With four kids you've got to be ready to handle anything." The minicrisis of Gran's ankle had pushed Max and Randall from her mind, but mentioning her children brought it all back in a rush.

Gran must have seen something in her face. "What's wrong, Kelly?"

Kelly rose, walked a few paces and sank into an overstuffed chair. "Nothing."

Geena, sitting opposite, brushed wispy auburn bangs off her face and looked Kelly over closely. "Yes, there is. Your eyes are swollen and red. You've been crying."

"Tell us what's the matter, Kel," Erin said.

Kelly stared into the empty fireplace, not knowing where to start. Then she released a deep sigh. "Max and I had a fight."

"Pass me my knitting, Geena, honey," Gran said in a low voice.

"Did you argue about your work again?" Geena asked sympathetically as she handed Gran a tapestry bag stuffed with yarn and needles.

"No..." Although she'd learned about Max's son two weeks ago, she hadn't yet confided in her sisters or Gran, hoping the whole nightmare would blow over. Now she could use some moral support. "Max had an affair the summer after high school with a girl on a dude ranch," she began, and went on to tell them the whole story.

"Oh, Kelly, sweetie," Geena said when Kelly finally finished. She put a hand over her sister's and squeezed. "This is dreadful. I can't believe he didn't tell you long ago."

"I can't believe this is Max we're talking about," Erin said, equally shocked. "You and he have been together since your junior prom."

Gran knit quietly. So quietly Kelly had to ask, "Did you know about the baby, Gran?"

Gran's soft brown eyes were thoughtful behind her oversize blue plastic glasses. Slowly, she shook her head. "No. And frankly, I'm surprised they managed to keep it quiet in a small place like Hainesville. At the time I did think it odd that Max and his parents were making so many trips out of town. I knew you were serious about Max so I was worried he was in some kind of trouble. But he went off to college as expected and nothing seemed amiss." She paused to count stitches, then turned her needles and started another row. "One thing I never doubted was that he loved you."

"He should have trusted her, too—enough to tell her the truth," Erin said.

"Well…he didn't want to risk losing me." Kelly caught herself defending him and hardened her voice. "And he was right to worry."

She slumped her aching head into her propped-up hand. "He invited Randall—that's his son's name—to stay with us for the summer…without even asking me!"

"You two need to sit down, calmly and rationally, and work through your problems," Gran said, glancing up from her knitting.

"How can she be calm when she's hurting so badly?" Erin demanded. "I love Max like a brother, but I think he's way off base for even suggesting a visit before clearing it with Kelly. It's adding insult to injury."

"He has put Kelly on the spot," Gran agreed. "What's the boy like?"

"I've only seen his photograph. He looks like a computer nerd. A *nice* nerd, mind you. Max feels sorry for him. He seems to think Randall won't be happy unless he takes the boy into his life. Into *our* lives."

"Perhaps if you give the child a chance, you'll like him, too," Gran suggested.

"I could never like a child of Max's by another woman," Kelly declared, propelled to her feet by the force of her emotions. "I know I'm not being politically correct or particularly nice, but that's how I feel.''

She paced to the window, half hoping she would see Max's car pull up outside. But the streetlight illuminated only the empty road and the broad limbs of the big maple that dominated Gran's front yard.

Her headlong flight into the night brought home the depth of her and Max's estrangement. Never before had she left the house in the middle of an argument. Always, she'd stayed to talk things through.

"Max has to meet her halfway," Erin said suddenly, as if reading Kelly's thoughts. "He has to make it up to her somehow."

"That's right," Geena agreed, staunchly supportive.

"Max'll never give in." Kelly returned to her seat. "He's so stubborn."

"Kelly, you can be just as obstinate," Gran pointed out, adding quietly, "sometimes more so."

"Max is set on getting to know his son," Kelly went on, ignoring that comment. "Randall's become the most important thing in his life, more important than me and the girls."

"I don't believe that for a moment," Gran said.

Deep down, Kelly didn't, either, but she was mad enough and hurting enough to *want* to think so.

"Now that he's found Randall he'll never let him out of his life."

The clock on the mantel chimed the hour. Geena made a move to gather up her sleeping baby. "I hate to leave you like this, Kel, but it's getting late. I have to take Sonja home and get some sleep before she wakes up again in four hours."

"I've got to go, too," Erin said, rising. "Nick was called out to a fire earlier and I told Miranda I'd only be half an hour. That was two hours ago." Her husband, Nick, was fire chief, and Miranda was his teenage daughter by a previous marriage. "Gran, maybe you'd better come home with me."

"I'll stay with her," Kelly said. "I don't want to go home, anyway."

"I'll make do just fine with that walking stick I used after my heart attack," Gran said. "You girls go home."

"You're going to need crutches even when you're allowed to be on your feet," Kelly said. "I'll stay," she repeated to Erin. "You and Geena can take off."

Erin bent to pick Erik out of the cot. The sleepy toddler rubbed his eyes with his fists. "I don't have to be at the bank tomorrow, so I'll come back first thing in the morning to stay with Gran while you go to work." Erin worked part-time at the Hainesville Bank as assistant manager.

"Tomorrow morning I volunteer at the seniors' center," Geena said. "I'll organize an appointment with Ben and Erin can take Gran to the clinic. It's settled," Geena said when Gran started to protest again. "Kel, do you want help getting Gran ready for the night?"

"We'll manage. And...thanks, you two, for listening."

Geena and Erin enveloped her in a three-way hug. "Take care, Kel," Geena told her.

"Everything will work out," Erin added. "You'll see."

"I hope so. Meanwhile I'd better call Max and tell him I'm staying here tonight to take care of Gran," Kelly said. "Tomorrow I'll go back to pack some of my things. Gran needs me and this is a good opportunity for Max and I to have some time apart."

After Erin and Geena left, Kelly got sheets out of the linen closet to make up the bed in her old room upstairs. When she'd done that she helped Gran to the bathroom and then into bed. "Promise you'll call if you need me in the night? That you won't try walking on that ankle?"

Gran nodded. "Just leave my bedside light on. I'm going to read awhile."

Kelly paused in the doorway. "Am I wrong for

not being more supportive of Max's need to know his son?''

Gran pushed her glasses up on her nose. "My dear, you can't help what you feel. Just don't lose sight of the most important thing in all this.''

"What's that?''

"You love Max, and Max loves you.''

TINA EYED THE BURNED TOAST and rubbery scrambled eggs Max set in front of her the next morning and stuck out her bottom lip. "Where's Mommy?''

"Yeah, where's Mom?'' Beth added. "She's supposed to drop me off at school early today. I've got softball practice.''

Kelly had only been gone one night, but already Max missed his wife. And it wasn't because she cooked eggs better than he did, or because her absence caused awkward questions. In thirteen years they hadn't spent a night apart, and he found he couldn't sleep without her curled next to him. Even though she'd called to say she was taking care of her grandmother, Max couldn't shake the feeling Kelly had used Ruth's injury as an excuse to stay away.

"I told you already,'' he said to Tina with diminishing patience.

"No, you didn't,'' Tina complained.

"You told me,'' Tammy piped up.

Bleary-eyed, Max blinked at his identical twin daughters in their identical Bugs Bunny pajamas. He didn't usually have trouble telling them apart, but this morning he felt as though he were seeing double. "She stayed at Gran's last night."

Tammy sipped at her orange juice. "Why?"

"Gran twisted her ankle and can't walk. She needs someone to help her."

"Mom's not coming back, is she?" Robyn's dark eyes, which reminded him so much of Kelly, were worried. She'd only picked at her breakfast.

"Of course she is," he replied automatically, but her question unnerved him. His eldest daughter was highly intuitive, but surely she couldn't know how deep the troubles lay between him and Kelly.

Then to his relief he heard the front door open and a moment later Kelly appeared, her small figure swirling into the kitchen with her usual energy.

"Good morning, girls," she said, not looking at Max.

Beth brightened, Robyn started eating, and Tammy and Tina immediately began complaining that the other one wouldn't wear the outfit she wanted to wear.

"Kelly…" Max began over the din.

"No one says you have to wear the same thing," Kelly said, ignoring Max to enter the fray. "Tammy, you put on your pink dress, and Tina can wear her purple overalls."

"But we *like* wearing the same clothes," Tammy and Tina said together, and off they went in the kind of circular argument that drove Max crazy.

"Kelly…" he said again.

"Beth, did you remember to pack your softball mitt?" Kelly continued as if he hadn't spoken. She took a cup from the cupboard and casually poured herself coffee.

"Yup," said Beth through a mouthful of toast and egg. She was naturally buoyant and oblivious to undercurrents; nothing stopped *her* from eating.

Max heard Kelly's cup clink against the coffeepot and noticed her hands weren't steady. She wasn't as blasé as she was pretending; like him, she had dark circles under her eyes.

"How is Gran's ankle?" Robyn asked.

"Pretty bad. I'll be staying there for a while."

"*What?*" Max exclaimed. "You said nothing of that last night."

Kelly stirred cream into her cup and took a sip. When she glanced up, the sorrow and a grim determination on her face frightened him. "I have to, Max. She can't walk on the foot. Geena and Erin will take turns looking after her during the day while

I'm at work, but they both have babies and new husbands and have to be home at night.''

''You have a husband and four children. You have to be home at night, too.''

''Gran needs me.''

''For how long?'' Max asked.

''Ben will give us a better idea after he examines her ankle, but it could be anywhere from four to six weeks, depending on how badly her ligaments are damaged. Come, girls. It's time to brush your teeth. I've got to get you to school and go to work myself,'' Kelly said.

Dragging their heels, the children went down the hall to their bedrooms and the bathroom.

Max grasped her slumping shoulders and turned her to face him. ''You can't seriously be planning to stay at Ruth's that long. The children need you.''

''I'll be here for the girls,'' she said, twisting out of his hands to reach for her purse on the table. ''I'll just go to Gran's to sleep.''

He moved with her, maintaining eye contact. ''*I* need you.''

Pain clouded her gaze, but she remained silent.

''This sprained ankle of your grandmother's came at an awfully convenient time.''

''If you're implying I'm lying, Ben will give you a full report—'' she began in umbrage, then broke off with a weary sigh. "Okay, it's not as bad as I've made out, but I don't want the kids to think we're having serious problems."

"I knew it. Ordinarily you would have looked at other options. Why don't you bring Ruth over here until her ankle heals?"

Kelly didn't speak for a moment; nor would she meet his gaze. "I was up half the night pondering what to do," she said at last. Tears swam in her eyes; impatiently she brushed them away. "I feel like I've shattered into pieces, Max. I have to get away for a while and put myself back together—if I can."

"We have to mend our marriage, Kelly, and we can't do that if we're apart."

Silence followed. Max heard their daughters' voices in the foyer as Tammy and Tina hunted for their shoes and Robyn and Beth packed lunches and books into their backpacks. The homely sounds of an ordinary school day provided a bitter counterpoint to the quiet desperation with which his world was falling apart. That he'd been the agent of destruction made it no less devastating.

"I need some time, and space," Kelly continued more quietly. "I need to be apart from you. I'd like to send *you* away, but I can't since your office is at home."

"For God's sake, Kel," Max said. "You've only

been gone a day and I miss you. If this is about Randall, I'll—''

''You'll what? Tell him he can't visit?''

Max shook his head, unable to deny his son.

Kelly nodded, lips compressed as she struggled to control her tears. ''This isn't easy for me, either, Max. Randall can come, but I won't stay in the same house. Afterward, we'll find out if there's anything left of our marriage.''

''It's no good having Randall if I don't have you.''

''Mom!'' Beth yelled from the front door. ''Are you coming?''

''Have you told the girls about him yet?'' Kelly asked in a more normal voice.

Max shook his head. ''I will tonight.''

''*Mom!*'' It was Robyn this time.

''I've got to go.''

Habit made Max reach for her; longing made him want to hold her. Before he could kiss her she slipped out of his arms with a quick decisive shake of her head. ''I can't.''

He followed her to the door, watching her glossy dark hair swing with each footstep, bouncing and gleaming in the sun streaming through the skylight. Even from this distance he could catch tantalizing whiffs of her lavender-and-vanilla shampoo, and his fingers itched to slide through those silky strands.

At the threshold she turned abruptly and his out-stretched hand fell to his side. "I'll come by after work to help with dinner and homework," she said. "And to pack my things." She was being quintessential Kelly now: brisk, efficient, emotions held firmly in check. "We won't tell the children we're separated unless we make it legal."

"We're not separated. You're staying at Ruth's to help out with her sprained ankle," he said, horrified by the speed at which she was leaving him.

"That's right." She nodded, approving his grasp of the story. "See you later."

And she was gone. Before he could so much as touch her cheek.

CHAPTER FIVE

AROUND NOON, KELLY FOUND a moment between clients to drop in at Gran's house. Geena and Erin had just returned from taking her to see Geena's husband, Ben, at the medical clinic.

"So what's the damage?" Kelly asked, coming into the kitchen. "Where's Gran?"

"Lying down," Erin told her. "The X rays showed no fractured bones, thank God."

"Ben says the ligaments are slightly torn, but not enough to require surgery," Geena added. "He put a splint on and told her to stay off her ankle."

Kelly felt relief, because her grandmother's injury wasn't as bad as it might have been and because she had a legitimate reason to stay away from home. Beth was engrossed in her sporting activities and the twins were too young to see through the flimsy story; only Robyn might figure out the truth. Well, if she asked, Kelly wouldn't lie.

"So tell us," Geena said, eyeing her curiously. "What happened with you and Max this morning?"

Kelly recalled the expression on Max's face just before she'd left the house—angry, pleading, frustrated and frightened. It was the way she felt inside. She'd had to overcome a physical urge to run back to the solid comfort of his arms, to hear his whispered assurance that everything would be okay. Instead, she'd bolted for the car. Everything was *not* okay, and never would be again, as long as Max insisted on bringing his son into their home. Randall would be a constant reminder of Max's affair—as if Kelly needed one—and a slap in the face to their marriage and their daughters.

"He asked me to come home," Kelly said. "I refused."

"Are you sure what you're doing is wise?" Erin asked. "If it came to a custody battle Max might claim you abandoned your children."

Kelly shook her head. "Max loves the girls too much to hurt them by denying me custody if we ever got divorced. That's one thing I'm sure of. Just as I would never deny him custodial rights."

"Surely it won't come to that," Geena protested.

"I hope not." Kelly felt suddenly bleak. As things stood between her and Max she couldn't be with him, but deep down she wanted nothing more than for their marriage to work.

Hours later, she turned in between the two tall cedars and drove up the long gravel driveway, having rescheduled a client so she could come home early and do some chores around the house.

She tiptoed past the closed door of Max's study, reluctant to encounter him and get into another fruitless argument. Into each of the girls' rooms she went, looking for dirty clothes. Theoretically, they were supposed to take their clothes to the laundry themselves, but it only worked out that way on Saturday during the weekly ritual of cleaning their rooms.

But even though it was Thursday she found no socks or underwear on the floor. No gym uniforms, no T-shirts with jammy fingerprints. In the laundry room, she opened the door and literally bumped into the reason why.

The bundle of clean laundry Max had just unloaded from the dryer tumbled onto the floor. ''What are you doing home?'' he demanded.

''Why aren't you working on your house design?'' Kelly stooped to help him pick up the clothes.

Their hands met unexpectedly between the folds of her silk nightgown and she yanked her hand back as an electric shock crackled from his fingertips to hers.

He gave her a slow smile. ''Guess there's some spark left.''

Kelly ignored the rush of heat caused by his brief

touch and straightened to start pairing socks. "It's called static electricity."

Max dumped his load of clothes on top of the dryer and wrapped his arms around her from behind. "Admit it, Kel. We belong together."

Kelly tried to concentrate on the ankle socks in her hand. Were they Beth's or Robyn's? Her eyes shut as he nudged closer, his thighs pressing against her bottom. He was right; they belonged together, and this was where she wanted to be—in his arms....

"*No.*" With an abrupt movement, she thrust her rear end backward, shoving him away, making him yelp. Spinning, she wagged a finger in his face. "No, no, no. You're not using sex to win me over, Max Walker. I'm not some lovestruck cheerleader and you're no longer a randy teenager. We've got issues! There'll be no sex, no foot rubs, no back scratches, no kissing or touching or pillow talk until we solve our problems."

"Okay," Max said grimly, withdrawing to cross his arms and lean against the washing machine. "Start talking."

She grabbed socks and underwear and tossed them into separate piles willy-nilly. "Not when you say it like that. I think we should see a marriage counselor."

Max threw his hands in the air. "You know how

I feel about spilling our personal problems to a stranger. It ain't gonna happen.''

"Andrea McCall is not a stranger," she said, referring to the family counselor in Hainesville.

"That just makes it worse. She's an old friend of my parents. You think I'm going to discuss my marital problems with her? She knows darn well my mother and father never wanted us to get married in the first place. That they thought our marriage would fail because we were too young. How am I going to feel when Andrea tells my mom she was right?''

Kelly shook her head. "Andrea is a professional. She wouldn't abuse client confidentiality."

"She saw me getting my diaper changed. I've exposed as much of myself to that woman as I'm ever going to." Max turned on his heel and stalked out of the room.

"There are other towns, other counselors," Kelly called after him, but he was gone.

Her arms fell slack at her sides. Drained by the up and down of emotions, Kelly finished sorting the clean laundry. After she'd distributed the piles to their respective rooms, she went into the kitchen to take chicken out of the freezer for dinner. The bouquet of dying roses still sat on the counter, petals wreathing the black granite around the base of the fluted glass vase.

Sighing, Kelly gathered the thorny stems and carried them out back to the compost bin. The Salish Lodge and that single magical night before she knew of Randall Tipton's existence seemed a lifetime ago. Was it only two and a half weeks ago she'd assured Robyn that she and Max would never split up? Or that they'd made love like newlyweds? Tears welled for her lost innocence, her dying marriage, her lost love. *Max, Max.* How could she bear to leave him? How could she stay?

She replaced the dead roses with long-stemmed bunches of blue and red anemones from her flower beds. On her way back to the house, she hesitated outside her plant room, where the arrangement she was making for a friend sat unfinished. She had no time today to work on it, but maybe this weekend.

Max came into the kitchen as she was browning the chicken pieces. "Erin's taking dinner over to Gran, so I'll stay and eat," she said. "I should be here when you tell the girls about Randall."

Her words brought relief to his tense expression. "Thanks," he said, briefly squeezing her forearm. "I appreciate that."

Damn him, she thought as he left the room. Damn him for making it so hard to stay angry. Seduced by his warmth and confused by her own mixed emotions, she felt a wave of compassion for him. Instead of simply baking the chicken in the oven, she added sour cream and mushrooms and turned it into the girls' favorite dinner.

IN THE END, MAX DECIDED he had to tell the girls on his own. He'd created the situation; he had to take full responsibility. While Kelly was busy cooking, he went looking for Tammy and Tina. Peeking unnoticed through the crack in the door of their room, he eavesdropped on their animated discussion.

Tina was kneeling on the carpeted floor, brushing her twin's curling blond hair with a doll's brush. "Wanna play dress-up, Tammy?"

"Yeah!" Tammy, cross-legged, her white undies showing beneath her dress, bounced on her bottom. "I'll be the fairy and you can be the princess."

"Okay. But we have to make a new crown, 'cuz Flora ate the last one." Tina got to her feet and went to the small table where they did "art." It was laden with scissors, paper, crayons, glue and tubes of colored sparkles—everything they needed to construct props for their games.

Tammy sat in the child-size wooden chair opposite and picked up a sheet of yellow construction paper and scissors. "I wish Mommy could help. She cuts the cardboard gooder than me."

Leaning over the table, Tina drew a line resembling mountain peaks across the yellow paper. "I hope Great-Gran gets better so Mommy will come back."

"Me, too." Tammy nodded in agreement. "Maybe if we be extra good she'll come home."

Unseen, Max made a face. He ought to go in now, but he couldn't resist watching the twins a little longer. Their make-believe games were endlessly fascinating, and in all honesty, he wanted to hear what else they had to say about their mommy.

Tammy cut along the jagged line, then laid the paper crown on the table. Tina colored in a giant central diamond while Tammy dabbed glue and gold sparkles over the rest of it. Then Tina taped the ends together and jammed it on her head.

Admiring herself in a doll's hand mirror, she declared it, "Beautiful."

Tammy eyed her sister judiciously. "It's a little crooked, but it's okay."

Tina headed for the toy box in the corner, where she pulled out Kelly's old prom dress and struggled into it; pink satin billowed around her feet. "I live in a castle and eat jelly doughnuts for breakfast," she announced. "You're my sister and you're coming to visit me because we're best friends."

Tammy stuck her arms through a pair of sparkly gauze-and-coat-hanger wings Kelly had made for

Halloween last year. "I fly in through the fairy door in the tower and give you a hug."

Tina's face clouded. "I miss Mommy's hugs."

Tammy reached up and adjusted Tina's crown. "Silly, she hugs us lots. Every morning and every night and when she picks us up from play school, and sometimes when you don't expect it."

"But when I woke up scared last night because of the monsters in my dream she wasn't there to hug me."

"No. That's true." Sad and thoughtful, Tammy kicked at the table leg. Then she brightened. "If the monster comes again, I'll hug you, okay, Tina?"

"And I'll hug you." Tina put her arms around her sister and they embraced, chubby cheek pressed against chubby cheek. "Now," Tina declared, all smiles, "let's have a tea party."

Max leaned against the wall outside their room, staggered at the effect his son was already having on his daughters' lives. Straightening, he knocked quietly, then pushed the door open when Tina's imperious princess voice bade him enter.

"Hi, girls—" He broke off, feigning surprise, and glanced around the room. "I thought my daughters were in here, but I see only a beautiful princess and an enchanting fairy. What have you done with Tina and Tammy?"

The girls giggled madly and shouted in unison, "It's us, Daddy!"

"So it is!" He lowered himself to the floor and patted the carpet to draw them near. "Sit down. I've got something important to tell you. We…we're going to have a visitor this summer."

"Marty?" Tammy asked hopefully, referring to Max's cousin who lived in Omaha.

"Er, no. Not Marty."

"Auntie Liz?" Tina suggested, meaning Kelly's aunt, who lived down the coast in Astoria.

"No…look, this isn't twenty questions." Max was getting flustered. "I'm trying to tell you who's coming. It's—"

"Sam!" both girls exclaimed, clearly overjoyed at the prospect of a visit from Max's wild and crazy college buddy, who came every second summer and stirred the girls into hysterics twenty-four hours a day.

"No." Max took a deep breath. "His name is Randall. He's thirteen and lives in Jackson, Wyoming."

He told them the rest in a few simple words. Only the facts, none of the whys or wherefores. They had an older half brother. He was coming to visit.

"Half brother?" Tina wrinkled her blond brow at the unfamiliar term. "Which half? Top or bottom?"

Max smiled. "My half. He's not your mother's son. He's another lady's son." They seemed to accept that, though goodness knows what they thought about it. "Do you want to ask me anything else?"

Tina adjusted the slipping crown on her head. "Where's he going to sleep?" she asked, always practical.

"He could sleep in my bed," Tammy said, "and I could share with Tina."

"Thanks. That's very generous of you, but I think we'll put him in Robyn's room and she can share Beth's bunk bed. I'd better go talk to them about it." He started to get up to leave, then paused. "I love you both. Come here. I want to hug you."

The girls scrambled across the floor and tumbled into his lap, two pairs of sweet little arms stretching around his neck. His voice thick, he squeezed them tight and told them, "Whenever either of you needs an extra hug you can always come to me if Mommy's not around."

Tina and Tammy exchanged solemn glances.

"When Gran's ankle is better, Mommy will be back," he hastened to assure them.

"Promise?" Tina asked.

"I promise." He loosened his grip and let them slide to the floor.

Now he just had to make that promise come true.

Max left them and walked down the hall to Beth's room. Again he knocked and waited till he was told he could enter. Beth was lying on her bed, reading by the light of a table lamp. She looked up, a question in her eyes, a finger marking her page.

"Hi, kiddo. Have a good day?" he asked, sitting in the computer chair at her desk. She nodded. "What did you learn in school today?"

"Nothing."

"You mean, you can't be bothered telling me about it," he said, smiling.

"No, I really didn't learn anything. We had a substitute teacher who gave us old work sheets to do."

"Oh." Max picked up one of her judo trophies, which were lined up on the bookshelf next to the desk. "How long have you been doing judo?"

"Three years," Beth said patiently. Her light ash-brown hair had the same springy texture as his. Tufts of it stuck out around the hem of the knit cap she'd jammed down around her ears in an attempt to flatten it. Try as she might to smooth out her hair with water or gel, it invariably bushed out around her head.

"What are you reading?" Max said, stalling, knowing she was waiting for him to get to the point.

She showed him a cover depicting a girl and a horse, then indicated two other books with bookmarks stacked on the floor beside her bed. "Those, too. But not right this second," she explained, literal minded as always.

"I've got something I want to talk to you about. Would you come out to the living room so I can talk to you and Robyn at the same time?"

"Can't you just tell me here?" Beth said, clearly wanting to get back to her book.

Max heard the distant sounds of Robyn practicing the same five or six notes over and over on the piano, trying in her determined perfectionist way to get the musical phrase exactly right. He couldn't go through this twice more. "No. Please come with me."

Robyn was still playing as they entered the sun-filled living room, which looked out on the side lawn through French doors. Her back was very straight and her hands moved over the keys with a fluid grace.

"Robyn."

She paused, fingers poised over the keys. "Yes?"

Max beckoned his eldest daughter away from the piano. She had Kelly's looks but his intuition. And she was a worrier. This time the telling wouldn't be so easy.

Sitting erect, Robyn folded her long, slender fingers in her lap. Beth sprawled across three-quarters of the couch, her legs dangling over the arm.

Oh, Lord, how was he going to spit this out? Max

took a deep breath. "There's something I have to tell you. I have a son, from before your mother and I were married."

"But, Daddy—" Beth frowned in confusion "—I didn't know you were married before Mom."

Man, this was getting harder and harder. "I wasn't. The girl and I were just…friends. She got pregnant, but her parents thought we were too young to get married so she gave the baby up for adoption. The boy's name is Randall Tipton and two weeks ago he wrote me a letter. I flew to Jackson to meet him last Saturday—"

"I thought you went to Seattle," Robyn broke in.

Caught out in a half truth. "Yes, well, I went to Seattle to catch the plane to Jackson." He was sweating now, under Robyn's steady, accusing gaze. "Anyway, I met Randall and his adoptive parents. He's a very nice boy and I'd like you girls to meet him."

"You mean we have a brother?" Beth asked, looking interested.

"*Half* brother," Robyn corrected her. "*I* don't want to meet him."

"I do," Beth said. "I think it will be cool to have a big brother. Does he play softball?"

"Not really," Max said, and Beth's face fell.

Somewhat desperately he added, "You could teach him. He'd be someone to play catch with."

"Is he going to live with us?" Robyn sounded appalled.

"No, just visit for the summer. How would you feel about bunking in with Beth when Randall comes at the end of June. Then he could have your room."

"No way! I'm not having a boy in my room, looking at my stuff, sleeping in my bed. Besides, Beth leaves her stinky sports socks lying everywhere." Robyn jumped up, outraged, her voice climbing higher with every sentence. "No, Dad. *No*. You can't make me."

Max counted to ten. "I *can* make you, but I'm hoping you'll be generous and welcome Randall to our home."

"Why should I? He's why Mom left you, isn't he?" Robyn stormed across the room and paused at the door to declare dramatically, "I'm never going to be nice to him. Never."

Max passed a hand over his face. When he looked up again, Beth was regarding him sympathetically. "Are you okay with this, Beth?"

She shrugged with her usual happy nonchalance. "Sure. He can have my room if he wants. But I'd rather share with the twins than with Robyn."

"Thanks, Beth, but we'll give Robyn a little time to come around."

"Dad?" she asked, suddenly frowning. "Mom hasn't really left us for good, has she?"

"No, of course not. She's in the kitchen now, making dinner." He got up and pulled her to her feet, slipping an arm around her shoulders. "Don't worry, sunshine. Everything's going to be okay."

Later, when the evening meal was over and the kids were in bed, Kelly went to the bedroom to pack more clothes while Max retreated to his office. Although he didn't see her go, he heard her: the click of the door, her footfall on the steps, the car engine coming to life, then receding in the night. If Kelly was trying to punish him she couldn't have come up with a better way to do it than by leaving him, over and over again.

MAX TOOK THE PASS FROM NICK and dribbled the basketball down the court, ignoring the shouts around him. He faked a pass to Ben, then leaped up to snag a neat slam dunk in the last few seconds of the game. They were playing in their regular Saturday-afternoon match: Hainesville versus Simcoe.

Breathing hard, Ben gaped at him. "Nice shot. Where's your head at, buddy?"

Nick, his other brother-in-law, laughed and

clapped him on the back. "With teammates like you, who needs an opposition?"

"Huh? What are you talking about?" Glancing around, he realized he'd put the ball in Simcoe's goal. Max swore under his breath and walked off the court to douse his head with water from a squirt bottle.

Ben came up behind him and threw an arm around his shoulder. "You okay, man? I've never seen your concentration break like that."

"I'm fine," he muttered, mopping his face with the hem of his T-shirt.

"Hey, Wrong-way Walker," Gerry, a plumber who played for Hainesville, joked. "Just for that, you're buying the first round at the Gillnetter."

"Ah, come on, Ger," Mike Travis, Simcoe's center, put in. "Don't hold it against Max." He grinned. "We would have won anyway."

Max shook his head, letting the good-natured ribbing from his teammates and their opponents wash over him. He just wished they'd all go.

With the authoritative ease of a fire chief used to giving orders, Nick moved the group of men away from Max. "Head on over to the tavern, fellas. We'll catch up with you in a minute."

"Thanks, buddy." Max sat heavily on a bench and pulled his sweaty T-shirt over his head.

"You look like you're not getting much sleep these days." Ben's assessing gaze was professional as well as brotherly.

Max shrugged and mopped at his damp chest.

Nick took a seat beside him. "We know Kelly's staying at Ruth's."

"How bad is Ruth's ankle?" Max hated checking up on Kelly's story but was unable to stop himself. "Is it that badly sprained?"

Ben nodded. "Given her age, I don't want her to walk on it for a few more weeks. She really does need someone with her."

"We also know about your son." Nick's gaze was sympathetic.

Max grimaced. "The whole town probably knows."

"I don't think so," Nick said. "Our wives share just about everything among themselves, but they don't gossip outside the family. Neither do Ben and I, so if you want to talk about Randall, you can. It's good that he got in touch with you."

"Kelly doesn't see it that way," Max said. "But he's my son. I can't turn my back on him."

"Of course you can't," Ben said. "It's a tough situation. Geena's worried about Kelly. Worried about you both."

"So is Erin," Nick added. "In fact, that's all I

hear about these days. Anything we can do to help, buddy?''

''At the moment, I'm coping.''

''Taking care of four kids must be a lot of work,'' Nick said, misunderstanding.

''The kids aren't the problem, and anyway, Kelly comes every day to help. In fact, she's doing more than *before* she left. But I miss her. Now I know the meaning of that expression, 'my other half.' I feel like my arm's been lopped off, or my leg.''

''Convince her to come home,'' Ben advised.

''Yes, but how? Short of breaking off communication with Randall, which I won't do.''

Nick bounced the ball between his feet. ''You've been married, what—thirteen years?'' Max nodded. ''Maybe a little romance would help. You know, like flowers and chocolates. Women love chocolate.''

Max's expression remained dubious. ''We just had a second honeymoon at Snoqualmie Falls. That was when all the trouble started.''

''It could be that Kelly's feeling insecure,'' Ben said. ''Even though your liaison with Randall's mother was long ago, it's new to her. I agree with Nick. Women like to be wooed. Now that she's living in her childhood home, you have a perfect opportunity to court her all over again.''

''It won't solve our issues over Randall,'' Max

said slowly. "But I guess it couldn't hurt…and it might get us talking constructively." Remembering their first night in the Salish Lodge, he brightened. "In fact, it might even be fun. Kind of recharge our relationship."

"That's the spirit." Nick clapped him on the back.

"Go get 'em, tiger," Ben said. "Now, who wants a beer?"

"Not for me," Max said, digging a clean T-shirt out of his kit bag and pulling it on. "I'm going to go ask my wife for a date."

CHAPTER SIX

"TRY ON THE SCHIAPARELLI, Kel." Geena held up a shocking-pink-and-black cocktail dress with matching beaded jacket.

Geena, a former model, kept some of her huge collection of clothes at Gran's. Saturday afternoon, she and Erin had come over to cheer Kelly up by playing dress-up. These days their childhood game had a grown-up twist: designer dresses.

"I don't know." Kelly gingerly touched the antique silk creation. "It looks so fragile."

"Oh, my God! You have a Schiaparelli?" Erin squeaked in awe. "I thought her designs were only in museums."

"The odd one comes up for private sale," said Geena, glowing in a ruby sequin sheath. "I was lucky enough to be in the right place at the right time. Come on, Kelly, try it."

"Okay, but don't blame me if I bust a seam." Kelly wasn't as fascinated by clothes as were Geena and Erin, but she enjoyed the time shared with her sisters.

She wriggled and shimmied and sucked in her tummy while Geena and Erin eased the delicate dress over her head and shoulders. It fit perfectly.

Geena stepped back and turned Kelly toward the full-length mirror on the cupboard door. Kelly stared, agog at the transformation the dress had made in her. She seemed a completely different person, elegant and mysterious. "Who *is* that woman?"

"You look stunning!" Geena exclaimed. "Doesn't she, Erin?"

"Like Greta Garbo." Erin, in a pearl-gray satin evening dress, was seated on a low stool, surrounded by a dozen or more pairs of shoes. She held up a pair of sparkly fuchsia slingbacks with very high heels. "These will go perfectly with that outfit. Try them on, Kel."

Kelly climbed into them and turned an ankle to inspect the shoes in the mirror. "They're gorgeous, but a bit too narrow and a lot too long," she said regretfully. "My feet slide forward."

Geena yanked a handful of tissues from the box on the dresser. "Stuff these in the toes."

Kelly did, and it helped, although the shoes still pinched. "I actually appear tall, for a change." She took a tottering step and had to grab Geena's shoulder for support. "How do you walk in these things?"

"You don't walk, sweetie—you summon a driver." Geena fussed with the collar of the jacket. "You're welcome to borrow the outfit anytime."

"Thanks, but I never go anywhere fancy enough to warrant wearing a dress like this."

"Maybe Max will take you someplace special to make up for Randall," Erin suggested.

"He's going to have to apologize before I'll go anywhere with him," Kelly replied. "You know, he hasn't once said he's sorry about his affair with Randall's mother. He seems to think that if he didn't *intend* to hurt me, then he doesn't have anything to apologize for. He's been like this since I've known him and I'm tired of it."

"'Never apologize, never explain' does seem to be some men's motto," Geena said. "But Max hardly ever does anything to apologize for, does he?"

"No, but that doesn't mean he should be let off the hook when he does," Kelly said. "I go over there every day, but we hardly speak to each other."

"I bet once Max realizes how much he misses you he'll do whatever it takes to get you back," Erin said, draping a Hermès scarf around her bare shoulders.

"You'd better decide what you're going to do when he does."

"Try ignoring him," Geena advised. "It makes men crazy. They can't stand to think they're not making an impression on you."

Downstairs the doorbell rang.

Erin picked up her skirts and hurried out of the room. "Don't you move, Gran," she yelled down the stairs. "I'll get it."

She was back a minute later bearing a large flat box wrapped in gold paper and a card with Kelly's name on it. "This was on the mat."

Kelly opened the card and her heart contracted at the flowing lines of a familiar signature. "'Sweets for my sweet, love, Max.'"

"Not terribly original, but it's a nice sentiment," Erin said.

Kelly tore open the wrapping. "Ooh, Godiva chocolates. Dig in."

"I really shouldn't," Geena said, and took two.

"He must have gone to Simcoe for these," Erin said, choosing dark chocolate. She sank her teeth into the soft center with a low moan. "They're fantastic."

Kelly ate one absently as she reread the card, recalling the love notes Max used to pin to the fridge. In the early days of their marriage he'd worked long hours to make ends meet. Now he was becoming successful, their girls were growing up happy and healthy and Kelly was feeling like a new woman with her job. How could their relationship fall apart just when everything else was coming together?

A cell phone rang. The three women scrambled among the pile of dresses and scarves, blouses and skirts heaped on the bed to locate the ringing device.

"It's mine." Kelly pushed a button to answer. "Hello?"

"Kelly?" Max said. "Hi."

Kelly held her hand over the mouthpiece and turned to her sisters. "It's Max. What should I do?"

"Tell him you'll call back when it's convenient," Geena suggested.

"No! Talk to him now," Erin admonished in a loud whisper.

Kelly rolled her eyes. "Hi, Max. Thanks for the chocolates. Is everything all right with the girls?"

"They're all fine. At least, I assume they are. Nancy's looking after the twins and Beth and Robyn are at friends' houses."

"So...what's up? Where are you?"

"I'm parked around the block. I, uh, I was wondering what you're doing tonight."

Kelly covered the mouthpiece again. "He wants to know if I'm busy tonight."

"Say you're available," Erin advised.

"Tell him you've got plans," Geena countered.

"Why, Max? Do you need me to be with the girls?" Please, God, don't let him be going out with another woman. Would he do that? No, surely not—

"There's a new movie playing in town," he said. "Do you want to go?" When she didn't answer right away, he went on. "We could stop by the Burger Shack first." Pause. "Or go someplace nicer."

Every cell in her body longed with a force beyond reason to say yes. Pride made her utter, instead, "Sorry. I can't." She glanced at her sisters, who were watching her avidly. "I...I'm doing something with Geena and Erin."

There was a long silence on the other end of the line. Kelly could feel his anger and disappointment as keenly as if he'd expressed it verbally. Seeking privacy, she walked out of the room and into Erin's old room next door and sat on the window seat. "Max, are you there?"

He grunted.

"Listen, Max. You can't just call me up and ask me for a date as if nothing's happened. We need to talk about our problems."

"You come home after work to spend a few hours with the girls, then rush off again. You never sit down long enough to talk with me. I'm trying to make that happen."

''We can't talk until—A, you apologize, and B, you agree to joint counseling.''

''For God's sake, Kelly, not that again.''

''Yes, that again. Randall has added a truckload of baggage to our already shaky marriage.''

''Our marriage has a strong foundation. It'll hold up.''

She didn't answer, couldn't think of any way over the impasse. The silence stretched until she started to think about how much this call must be costing them. ''Was there anything else?''

''Actually, yes,'' Max said. ''I had a favor to ask, but now I doubt you'll agree.''

''Try me,'' she said, wary but willing to listen. They might be estranged, but they still had a responsibility to each other.

''Randall's arriving later this month—''

''Oh, no. Not that. Max, don't ask me—''

''I'd really like his adoptive parents to gain a good impression of the home he's going to be staying in.''

Agitated, Kelly swung her legs off the window seat and paced across the room. ''I want no part of that boy.''

''Kelly, you've got to be home when they arrive. You've got to pretend nothing's wrong between us. Please.''

''Max—''

"If you won't do it for my sake, what about our daughters? Think how awkward it will be for them if Marcus or Audrey Tipton asks them why their mother isn't home. We've taught them not to lie, Kel."

"I'm away because I'm looking after my grandmother."

"I really think the Tiptons would be more comfortable leaving Randall in a two-parent household. Please. I...I'm begging you."

Kelly was mildly shocked. Max *never* begged.

"All right, I'll do it," she agreed reluctantly. But it wasn't for Max's sake, or even the girls. She would do it for the boy. He wasn't to blame for the situation and she would play no part in hurting an innocent child.

"Thanks, Kelly. "I really appreciate—"

"I don't want your thanks," she said, cutting him off. "Just don't ask me to like him."

RANDALL FELT INSTINCTIVELY that the woman greeting him resented his presence in her home, but he told himself he was imagining things and politely held out his hand. "How do you do, Mrs. Walker?"

"Fine. Thank you." She took his hand briefly and dropped it again quickly. She didn't ask him to call her by her first name, as Max had.

Randall lowered his gaze, discreetly checking to see if his fly was done up and that he had no stains on his shirt. Everything seemed to be in order. Max frowned slightly at his wife, and her lips curved in a frozen smile that made Randall feel even worse.

His mom and dad didn't seem to notice anything wrong, possibly because they were nervous themselves. His mom had gotten embarrassed when the men had had to lift her wheelchair over the steps into the house. Randall walked behind her as they moved through the spacious, light-filled rooms, keeping a hand on her shoulder. Whether it was for her comfort or his, he couldn't have said.

"Nice house," Marcus remarked to Max as they were shown the living room. "Did you design it yourself?"

"Yes," Max replied. "I also worked on it from the ground up, helping the carpenters, plumbers and electricians wherever I could. Too many architects don't know the practicalities of the building trades and it shows in their designs. Plus, we couldn't have afforded the place otherwise. Kelly decorated. She's got a great eye for color."

"I agree," Audrey said, swiveling her chair for a better look at an arrangement of dried flowers and grasses on a side table.

Randall touched a fingertip to the delicate rigging

on one of three model ships lined up along the mantelpiece.

"My grandfather, who was a fisherman, made those," Max told him. "He carved the pieces by hand during winter when the salmon weren't running."

"They're really good," Randall said, admiring the workmanship and the patience required to build such ships. It occurred to him as they moved on that Max's grandfather was his great-grandfather and that gave him a funny feeling in his chest. At the doorway he paused to glance back at the model ships.

Max rested a hand lightly on his shoulder. "Coming? I want you to meet your half sisters."

The family room overflowed with girls. Two small ones were laughing and racing around the coffee table, a pair of large dogs at their heels. A girl with bushy light brown hair grinned at him from the depths of an armchair and an older one who looked about his age stood with her arms crossed and gave him an icy stare that reminded him of Mrs. Walker. Randall felt his face heat and dug his fingers into his mother's shoulder. She placed her cool, dry, comforting hand over his.

"Tina, Tammy, stop running around and say hello to the Tiptons," Max said. The twins halted abruptly, stared at Randall and giggled their hellos. "And these are our elder daughters, Robyn and Beth. Girls, maybe you'd like to take Randall outside and show him around.''

The eldest girl gave her father a furious look. The middle girl, who looked friendly, asked, ''Do you want to play catch?''

''Uh…'' Randall had never owned a baseball mitt. He'd had to play the sport in school, but he'd never been good at it. The backyard was fully visible through huge windows. If he went out there with Beth and tried to throw the ball around he'd look like an idiot in front of Max and everybody.

''Randall has asthma,'' Audrey interjected. ''He can't run around. Did you bring your ventilator, Randall?''

He flushed and sent his mom an agonized glance. ''I grew out of asthma two years ago.''

Cripes. Sometimes she treated him as if he were breakable. She'd fretted all the way here about whether ''these people'' would be suitable temporary guardians for him. ''That's what we're going to find out, Audrey,'' his father had said. ''If we don't feel comfortable with the situation, we'll make some excuse and take Randall home.'' Those words had sent Randall into a cold sweat.

The golden dog trotted over and snuffled at his ankles. Grateful for the distraction, Randall dropped to his knees to scratch behind its ears. "Hey, boy, what's your name?"

"Billy," one of the little girls said.

"The black doggie is Flora," the other twin added. "She's a girl."

Marcus sneezed, as if on cue. Sneezed again and again. "Sorry, it's my...achoo!...allergies."

"Tammy, Tina, take the dogs outside, please," Max said, and the little girls ran through the sliding doors onto the lawn, the dogs bounding after them. Randall watched them go regretfully.

With the removal of the dogs and younger girls, an awkward silence fell over the group. Audrey searched her handbag for Marcus's allergy medication.

"I could use a cup of coffee," Max's wife said. "How about you folks?"

Automatically polite, Randall asked, "Would you like some help, Mrs. Walker?"

She gave him an odd glance, as if not quite sure whether he was sucking up or just a weirdo. "No, thanks," she said, moving over to the island bench, where cups and a plunger pot were already laid out. "I just have to put on the kettle."

"Robyn, now might be a good time to show Randall his room. You and Beth could help him bring in his things."

Sullen-faced, the older girl turned on her heel without a word and left the room. Randall hesitated. The last thing on earth he wanted to do was follow her, but he guessed he had no choice.

"Come on, Randy," Beth said cheerily. "Let's go."

It took him a second to realize she was talking to him; no one had ever called him Randy before, not even the kids at school. He decided he kind of liked it.

"Don't worry about Robyn," Beth added as she led him down the hall and out the front door. "She's just mad because she has to share with me while you're here."

So that was why she was being such a pain. But Beth was nice, really nice. How could her sister mind sharing? If he had a brother, he'd like nothing better than to share a room with him. They could stay up late, talking....

"You don't say much, do you?" Beth chatted on. "Dad says sometimes I talk *too* much, mostly when he's trying to concentrate on the news on TV. But Mom always listens—when she's home, that is. Oops. Um, I mean... Hey, cool car."

"It's just a Lincoln Continental. Dad trades it in every two years for a new one." Then he noticed their older-model station wagon and even older sedan sitting in the driveway. He shrugged. "It's no big deal."

Robyn had the trunk open and was struggling with a large cardboard box.

"I'll get that." Randall hurried over. "It's my computer. You could take that suitcase. If you don't mind, that is." She rolled her eyes, and he started to sweat. "Thanks," he mumbled.

Robyn dragged the black suitcase from the car, bumping it over the driveway and back into the house. Randall grimaced. His mom had bought the suitcase especially for this trip; she wasn't going to like seeing it come home battered.

"You've got your own computer?" Beth asked, clearly in awe. "That is so cool. Do you have any good games?"

"Oh, yes," he replied, pleased to find a fellow aficionado. "I'm in the middle of a very exciting chess tournament on the Internet."

Beth wrinkled her nose. "I mean fun games, like Monkey Island and Lords of Magic." She picked up a narrow box. "What's in here?"

"That's the printer. It's got to stay upright."

They took their load back into the house and down a corridor that led off the hallway to a bedroom that overlooked the side yard and rows and rows of flowers.

The room was painted lavender and held a single bed with a ruffled floral coverlet and a pink-painted dresser. Ruffled curtains matched the coverlet, and on the wall was a poster of the New York City Ballet and a framed print of a Degas ballerina. A pair of bronzed ballet shoes hung from a hook beside the mirror over the white dresser. Randall hadn't felt so uncomfortable since he'd accidentally stumbled into the girl's bathroom in grade two.

He set the computer down on the desk. "Thanks for letting me use your room," he said to Robyn.

"It's not like I had a choice." She flicked her straight brown hair behind her ear. "The right-hand drawers on the dresser are empty. You can put your stuff in there, and you can use the top drawer of the desk. Don't open any other drawers or look through my things in the closet. Do you understand?"

"Yes. Thanks. You can use my computer if you want."

Robyn sniffed. "I doubt I'll want to do that."

"I would," Beth piped up.

"Sure." Randall smiled at her. "Anytime."

"Don't be so stupid, Beth," Robyn hissed at her. "He may be our half brother, but he's not our friend." She transferred her attention to Randall, and he was so startled by the ferocity of her gaze he stepped backward. "I'm not even going to pretend I like you. I don't want you here, and the sooner you go back where you belong, the better.''

''Robyn!'' Beth gasped.

''Well, gosh,'' Randall said, bewildered and hurt and finally stung into anger by her meanness. ''If your room is so important to you, I'll sleep on the couch.''

''It's not the room,'' she said scornfully. ''Although I'm not happy about that, either.''

''What is it, then? Our father?'' She winced, and he wished he'd chosen different words. ''I'm not trying to move in permanently.''

She sent him a final scathing glance. ''You don't know anything. My mom moved out when she heard you were coming. *You* are the reason my mother and father are separated. If they get divorced, that will be all your fault, too!''

As Randall gaped at her, her brown eyes went liquid and she spun on her heel to run from the room. He turned to Beth. ''Is that true?''

She looked miserable and shrugged. ''Mom's been staying at Great-Gran's house for over a month. We don't know when she's coming back.''

Oh, man. ''I didn't mean to cause trouble.''

''It's not your fault.''

But Robyn wouldn't hate him that much unless it *was* his fault. That settled it. He would go back with his parents. Dad would wonder, but Mom would be too pleased to make a fuss, or care why he'd changed his mind.

Randall left the computer in its box for the moment and went back to the family room, determined to get his dad alone and tell him he didn't want to stay after all. Marcus could make whatever explanation he thought best.

But then Max glanced up and smiled at him and his resolve wavered. There were so many things he wanted to know that only Max could tell him. If he left now, he probably wouldn't get a second chance.

"Randall," Max said, "I was just saying to your parents that I'd like you to work for me this summer."

"W-work for you? Doing architecture stuff?" He'd never dreamed of having such an opportunity.

"Mostly gofer tasks, I'm afraid, but I can show you how to use AutoCAD software if you're interested. You could be a big help and you'll make some spending money. Since Kelly started working I've been in dire need of an assistant, even more so now that my business is expanding. What do you think?"

"I'd love to!" Randall blurted without considering. "That would be so cool."

"Your eldest daughter doesn't help you?" Marcus asked.

"Oh, she would if I insisted, but she's got so much going on with ballet and piano and friends. I thought Randall might like something to occupy him." Max smiled easily. "Don't worry, though, I'm not a slave driver. He'll have plenty of time for himself. We'll take him to the beach and out on the river. There's fishing and miles of trails to explore in the woods with the dogs. And if I know my Beth, she'll have him playing ball before the summer's out."

"You paint a very welcoming picture," Audrey said, then turned to Kelly. "Another child in the house will mean a lot of extra work. Are you sure you don't mind Randall being here?"

Randall's breath caught and his blood began to race. Now. Now was the time to speak. Before *she* said it. But his throat seemed paralyzed and he couldn't get a sound past his lips.

Kelly Walker was sitting on the same couch as Max, but there was a good foot of charcoal-colored upholstery between them. Now she reached across and took his hand, and smiled at Audrey. "Of course not," she replied warmly. "One more child is no bother. I'm just so pleased for Max that he's able to get to know his son. We'll all enjoy having Randall."

She *looked* sincere. She *sounded* sincere. Max was gazing at her with something close to adoration. Randall was confused. He glanced around to gauge Beth's reaction, then saw her, outside on the lawn, throwing a stick for the dogs.

"Well," Marcus said, glancing at his wife. "We should probably be going if we're going to make it to your sister's in Seattle by dinner. Are you ready, dear?"

Audrey gazed at Randall with a tremulous smile. "Ready as I'll ever be. This is the first time Randall's been away from home except for a week at summer camp."

"I'll be fine, Mom." He hoped. For weeks he'd been looking forward to this vacation with unadulterated pleasure. Now he felt unsure of himself and his place in this house.

"He's welcome to call home anytime," Max assured them. "And should he get homesick and want to leave…well, we'll cross that bridge if we come to it."

Max and Randall walked his parents out. Randall swallowed the lump in his throat as he said goodbye to his parents and hugged them. He'd set this train of events in motion and now he wasn't so sure he wanted to ride it to the end. Too late. They were pulling out of the driveway, his mom waving through the window. Waving, waving, and then…gone.

"So…" Max turned to him. "I guess you'll want to finish setting up your room."

"Yeah, sure."

As they were going inside, Kelly came out carrying an overnight bag. Frowning, Max caught her arm and she stopped, strained lines etching her mouth.

"Go on, Randall," Max said to him, and Randall moved into the house, a bad feeling in his stomach.

At the corridor that led to the bedrooms he paused and peeked around the corner. Max and Kelly were visible through the open door, and although they were speaking in low tones, Randall could hear every word.

"Are you taking your entire wardrobe over there?" Max said. "How long are you planning on staying away?"

"As long as necessary," she replied stiffly.

"None of this is necessary." Max touched her cheek and she moved her head. She looked impatient to leave; Max seemed just as reluctant to let her go. "Thanks for coming today," he added. "Randall's a nice kid, isn't he?"

"He's certainly polite." Kelly paused. Then, clearly distressed, she spoke her next words in a rush. "Max, I can't discuss him as though he were a neighbor kid or one of the girls' friends. You're just going to have to accept that. I did what you asked. Don't expect any more of me.''

''Okay, Kel,'' Max said, pain evident in every quiet syllable. ''Okay.''

Randall melted back around the corner, too upset to listen to any more. This was too awful. He *was* responsible for the trouble between Max and Kelly. Maybe they would even get divorced, as Robyn feared.

CHAPTER SEVEN

KELLY WALKED IN TO WORK from Gran's house on Monday morning. Orville Johannson waved to her from the door of his barbershop and Rosa's cheery face beamed at her from between the hanging salamis in the display window of her delicatessen. Mayor Gribble and banker Jonah Haines stood on the corner of Main and Elm, debating the finer points of fly-fishing. Birds sang, children laughed and all of Hainesville seemed to glow in the summer sun.

Kelly wasn't glowing. She'd risen late after a sleepless night and was tired and irritable. She shed her sweater at the door of the real estate office and wiped a faint sheen of perspiration from her hairline. The temperature must be in the eighties already. Her flowers were going to wilt.

Ray hurried out of his office, his patience as thin as his cheap blue suit. "Where've you been?" he demanded, pointedly gazing at a flashy gold-colored watch. "It's nine-twenty." She started to speak, but he waved her apology away. "Never mind. We've got a couple interested in the Harper house—Hal and Marjorie Woolridge. They'll be here in ten minutes." He pointed a stubby finger at her. "You mention the leaky roof again and—"

"If you don't like the way I work with clients, why don't you show them the house yourself?" She'd loved this job at first, but in the past year had found Ray increasingly hard to take. Not that she could ever admit as much to Max after she'd fought so hard at first to get the job and then to keep it. Whatever else she was, Kelly was not a quitter. And she hated to hear the words *I told you so*.

"I've got another appointment," Ray said. "I'm going to be late myself if I don't get moving." He gave her an oily smile as he adjusted his tie. "Word around town says you left Max."

"I'm looking after my grandmother, who has a sprained ankle," Kelly said firmly. Ever since his divorce Ray had been hitting on anything with two X chromosomes. He'd been annoying enough when she and Max were together; she shuddered to think how he'd behave if he thought she was free.

His eyes narrowed, Ray seemed to be assessing whether or not she was being completely truthful, and if not, what his chances were. "If you'd like some company some night…"

"Goodbye, Ray." Ray shrugged and went out the

door. Kelly turned to Annette, the pretty blond receptionist typing a letter at the front desk. "Hi, Annette. Any messages?"

"I put them on your desk." Taking her gaze off the computer to look at Kelly, Annette added, "How are you?"

"So-so." Kelly leaned on the counter. "Tell me, Annette, why doesn't Ray ever make a pass at you?"

"He was very persistent when I first started working here," Annette admitted. "Finally I said yes, just to get him off my back. When he asked me where I wanted to go for dinner, I told him the name of the most expensive restaurant in Seattle." She smiled at the memory. "It was a wonderful meal. Poor Ray paid the bill without a peep, but that was the last time he asked me out."

"Wow." Kelly shook her head in admiration. "I'm surprised he didn't, you know, expect something from you in return."

"Oh, he did." Annette smiled as she turned back to the computer. "Not many people are aware I have a black belt in karate."

Kelly snorted with laughter and went around the dividing wall to her office. The room was just a cubicle, really, because the walls didn't reach the ceiling, but the space was *hers*. Maybe real estate wasn't her dream profession, but she'd come a long way since she'd obtained her license and learned the skills necessary to be a successful agent. Not, she acknowledged with a frown, that Ray would consider her successful.

She had a few minutes until the Woolridges arrived so she booted up her computer and checked her e-mail. Skimming through the dozen or so messages she found nothing from Max. After the chocolates and the movie invitation, she'd secretly hoped he might contact her again. In the past they'd often e-mailed messages back and forth.

Kelly, could you stop at the printers? Love you, babe. Sure, Max. Remember to take the hamburger meat out of the freezer. Love you right back.

Those days of easy loving already seemed long ago. She glanced at the framed photo on her desk of Max and the girls. She couldn't understand how she could be so angry with him and yet miss him so much. "Why, Max?" she whispered, stroking a fingertip across his image. "Why aren't the girls and I enough?"

Pushing her disappointment to the back of her mind, Kelly clicked on Compose Message. *Max,* she wrote, *could you please water my flowers?* Her fingers hovered over the keys, itching to tap out *Love you.* With a brisk shake of her head, she hit Send, instead.

Her phone rang. It was Annette, saying Mr. and Mrs. Woolridge had arrived for their ten o'clock appointment. "I'll be right out."

She spun on her chair to retrieve the dog-eared binder of property listings from the credenza, then went out to greet a casually dressed couple who looked to be in their late forties. "Hi. I'm Kelly Walker. I understand you're interested in a five- or six-bedroom house."

"That's right," Hal said. "We're looking for a place we can semi-retire to."

Kelly led them into her office and gestured to them to have a seat. Turning her book of listings so they could see the photograph, she said, "The Harper house is one of the original farming homesteads in the area, built about 1865. It's the only six-bedroom house on our books at the moment. The property is lovely—five acres with river frontage—and is well located between Hainesville and Simcoe."

"Sounds pretty good," Hal agreed. "Has the house been on the market long?"

"Awhile," she admitted, an understatement considering the house had been up for sale for nearly three years. "We don't have much demand for six-bedroom houses."

"The asking price seems quite low," Marjorie said. "Lower than many smaller homes in this area.

Ray spoke about it in such glowing terms I don't understand. Could he have given us the wrong figure?''

''The asking price *is* low,'' Kelly said, ''but the figure Ray gave you is correct. Where did you folks say you were from?''

''Florida,'' Hal replied. ''We want to move north and open a bed-and-breakfast.''

''Hainesville would be a perfect spot for a B and B,'' Kelly enthused. ''There's only one other in town.'' She leaned forward, hands clasped. ''I grew up in Hainesville and I can't say enough good things about the area. It has the best of small-town living with a large city on our doorstep. We've got beaches, the river, fishing, mountains nearby—something for everyone.'' *And for you nice folks a white elephant of a house in desperate need of repair.*

Hal and Marjorie exchanged pleased glances. ''What are the schools like?'' Marjorie asked. ''We've got a couple of teenagers.''

''My kids are still in primary school, but my step-niece, Miranda, goes to the high school and loves it. She and my brother-in-law Nick, who's the fire chief in Hainesville, came from L.A. just over a year ago. I'm sure she'd help your kids with the transition.''

''We're also looking at a place near Bellingham,'' Hal told Kelly. ''It's not as big, but it's ready to move into. What kind of shape is your Harper house in?''

Oh, boy. Ray would fire her if she screwed up another sale. She'd love to tell him to stuff his job, but if she did separate from Max, she would need the work. On the other hand… Kelly looked from Hal to his wife. Hal had an easygoing, lived-in sort of face, and Marjorie had a quiet, friendly manner. She'd liked them at first sight.

Taking a deep breath, she smiled apologetically. ''The house has a few structural problems. The roof leaks and the foundations need repair. Termites, you know. There are a few other problems, too. They're all fixable, and the owners are negotiable on the price, but unless you're a tradesman or have money to spend…'' She lifted her shoulders, as sorry for herself as for them, ''I couldn't in good conscience advise you to go further with this house.''

Hal exchanged another glance with Marjorie. ''I'm a carpenter,'' he told Kelly. ''We're looking for an older house we can buy cheaply and do up.''

''Hal can fix anything,'' Marjorie assured her, patting her husband's knee proudly.

''Wonderful!'' Relieved, Kelly let out a burst of laughter and rose to her feet. ''What are we waiting for? Let's go see the house. But do me a favor? Don't tell my boss I mentioned the roof.''

MAX HAD A SITE INSPECTION in the morning on Whidbey Island. When he returned at lunch he found Randall setting up the sprinkler on Kelly's flower beds.

"Hi, Randall," he called, coming out of the sliding doors leading from the family room. "Thanks for watering the flowers. It's going to be hot today."

To Max's surprise, Randall's cheeks turned red. "I was sorting your e-mail like you wanted me to and there was a message from Mrs. Walker, asking you to do it. I wasn't snooping, honest, but it was only one line so it was right there on the screen."

"That's okay, Randall. I'm sure she'll appreciate it." He paused. "Did her e-mail say anything else?"

"No." Randall shook the water off his hands rather than wipe them on his pants, as any of his other kids would have done. He glanced at Max, then down at his feet. "I couldn't help notice Mrs. Walker was a little angry when she left last night. I...I hope I'm not in the way. If you think I should leave, just tell me."

"Jeez, Randall, no." Max shoved a hand through his hair. "Kelly's just..." How much did you tell a thirteen-year-old, no matter how mature he seemed? As little as possible, he decided. "Kelly's taking care of her grandmother. She'll be back when her Gran's foot is better."

"Sure," Randall said, but he appeared unconvinced. "I finished the photocopying and filing. The mail came—I put it on your desk. Oh, and a woman from the Simcoe School of Dance called and wanted to confirm your Latin-dance lessons starting this Thursday evening."

Max hadn't been that keen on Latin dancing in the beginning, but now he would gladly participate, if only to see Kelly. However, if she wouldn't take in a movie with him, there seemed little chance she'd accompany him dancing.

"The lessons were an anniversary gift from Kelly to me," he told Randall. "But she doesn't want— isn't *able* to attend now that her grandmother needs looking after. I'd better call and cancel."

"If they were an anniversary gift, you should go," Randall protested. "I could stay with her grandmother."

"Randall, I don't want you feeling guilty over what's going on with Kelly and me." He squeezed the boy's shoulder. "Say, you've been working hard and deserve a break. Why don't you take my fishing rod and head down to the dock."

"I'd like that, but..." Randall momentarily brightened at the suggestion, then he shrugged and fell silent.

As Max studied Randall's downcast expression, it

dawned on him that maybe the boy didn't know how to fish. "What the heck. You've been such a help today I can afford to take an hour or two off."

Randall's grin spread across his freckled face. "Great."

"I'll get the rods. You run in and shut down the computer, okay?"

"Sure thing."

Randall hurried inside to the office. He touched the mouse and the screen saver disappeared, revealing the in-box. Guilt washed over him anew at the sight of Kelly's e-mail. No matter what Max said, it was obvious Max and Kelly were fighting because of him. And now, also because of him, they'd have to cancel their plans to learn Latin dancing. It just wasn't right.

But there was nothing *he* could do about it....

Unless he replied to Kelly's e-mail with a reminder of the upcoming lessons.

His heart suddenly pounding, Randall glanced at the doorway. This felt sneaky and wrong. But would it be wrong if Kelly and Max got back together as a result? When his school debating team had argued the pros and cons of the question "Does the end justify the means?" Randall had been on the pro side, arguing there were occasions when a positive outcome justified dubious means. Randall wasn't quite sure he believed that, but his team had won, and undoubtedly he could come up with a convincing argument for the present set of circumstances, too.

However, if his plan failed, he could make things worse....

Shut up, Tipton. You're not in a debate now.

Seating himself at the computer, Randall quickly typed in a message.

Dear Kelly, I watered your flowers as you asked. Don't forget, Latin-dance lessons start this Thursday.

Randall's fingers hovered over the keys. If he said Max would pick her up, then he'd have to get Max over there somehow. Better to get her to come here.

Can you drive? My car is broken.

Randall frowned at the screen. That sounded neither convincing nor chivalrous. Then he heard Max's footsteps in the hall.

"Randall? Are you coming?"

"Right away," he called. No time to edit the message. But how to finish?

Your loving husband, Max.

Before he could worry about the wording or the ethics of his actions, Randall hit Send. A moment later he clicked out of the e-mail browser and started the shutdown procedure.

Max appeared in the doorway, carrying a tackle box and a pair of fishing rods. "Everything okay?"

"Sure. Fine." Sweat dampened Randall's armpits, but he thought his voice sounded reasonably collected. "I, uh, took care of the dance lessons. You don't need to worry about canceling."

Max's eyebrows rose. "You didn't have to do that. But thanks. I guess."

"No problem. Anything I can do to help." Randall pressed the off switch and moved away from the computer. So far, so good.

"Let's go," Max said, then paused to stare at Randall, frowning hard.

Randall swallowed. "Something wrong?"

"You can't sit on a mossy dock in those good shorts. Don't you have any cutoffs?"

Breathing out carefully, Randall said, "No, sir."

"You're almost as tall as I am. I'll lend you a pair."

"I would appreciate that very much, sir."

Max clapped him on the back in a friendly manner and shook him a little as if to loosen him up. "What did I tell you about calling me sir?"

"Not to do it. Sir."

Max opened his mouth, then saw the hint of a twinkle in Randall's eye. Well, what do you know, the kid had a sense of humor. He laughed out loud. "Come on, you."

A half an hour later, he and Randall sat, rods in hand, in companionable silence on the edge of the dock, their bare feet dangling above the water. Dragonflies buzzed around the reeds in the shallows, and overhead the deep blue sky was rimmed with towering white clouds. Max thought of all the work he should be doing, then mentally shrugged. If a man didn't pause to enjoy life occasionally, what was the point of it all?

"This isn't the best time of day for fishing," Max said after a lazy while. "But it's the best time for sitting on a dock in the sun."

"It's very peaceful," Randall agreed.

"Is the fishing good around Jackson Hole?"

"I guess so. I've never been," Randall replied. "Father doesn't fish. He's very good at golf, though. He was going to teach me this summer, but—" Randall fell abruptly silent.

"Randall, I didn't realize. I'm sorry you missed out on that."

"It doesn't matter." Randall pulled tentatively on his rod, watching the line tighten with the drag of the water.

Something about the quality of his silence made Max ask, "Are you homesick?"

"A little." Then he met Max's gaze and a smile touched his eyes. "But I'm really glad to be here with you."

Max's chest seemed to expand. "I'm glad, too," he said, his voice gruff with emotion. "How are you getting along with the girls? They're not making you feel left out, are they?" Contrary to his expectations, Randall retreated to his room a lot in the evening.

"No. I don't talk to Robyn much, but Beth and Tina and Tammy are nice." He paused and lifted one shoulder slightly. "I guess I'm not used to being around so many people."

Suddenly Randall's rod jerked in his hands and the line pulled taut. Caught off balance, he nearly fell off the dock in his excitement. "I got a bite!"

"Steady. Hold it steady." Max resisted the urge to take the rod out of the boy's hands. "Reel in slowly. That's right. Keep it coming…"

A silver shape winked below the dark surface.

"There! Did you see it?" Randall shouted, as enthusiastic as a six-year-old. "I caught a fish!"

"You haven't got it yet. Tug on the line to make sure that hook's dug in well. That's it. Keep reeling." Max was on his feet, reaching for the net.

There was a thrashing and a splashing as the salmon broke the surface. River water sprayed in sparkling drops around the fish twisting and flapping on the end of the line.

Randall, his eyes and mouth wide with astonishment and delight, hauled on the tightly curving rod while with a deft scoop Max netted the wriggling fish.

"Whoo-hoo!" Randall whooped. "We got him!"

Max grinned. "That's a sockeye. Must be three or four pounds. Good going, kiddo."

He handed Randall the small wooden club he used to dispatch landed fish. "He's your fish. It's up to you to put him out of his misery."

Randall blanched, his freckles standing out starkly on his skin. "You mean…?"

Max nodded.

His mouth set in a grim line, Randall took the club, and a moment later, the salmon lay still. Randall was silent as he gazed down at the fish, and Max sensed the complex emotions running through him. He put a hand on Randall's shoulder. "You did good, son."

Randall's eyes met his. "Thanks."

Max knew Randall was thanking him for more than the compliment and his heart felt full. He smiled, grateful for this day and the shared experience.

"Fishing must run in your blood," he said as he put the salmon in the cooler. "Your great-grandfather on my father's side was a commercial fisherman."

"Is he the one who built the model ships?" Randall took a baby squid from the bait bucket and threaded it through the hook just as Max had shown him earlier.

Max looked on, feeling ridiculously proud. You didn't have to tell this boy anything twice. "That's right. He was one of the early settlers in this area." Max rebaited his own hook and cast his line back in the middle of the swiftly running river. "His name was Maxwell Walker, just like me. When I was a kid he told me stories about the old days. Literally millions of salmon came up this river every year on their way upstream to spawn."

"Wow. I'd like to have seen that." Randall gazed dreamily across the water. "How come you didn't end up fishing for a living?"

"My dad was a builder. He used to take me around construction sites from an early age. I loved seeing a structure grow from the ground up, going from nothing but an idea on paper to a home for a family.'' Building a house was kind of like building a family, Max had always thought. With solid foundations, like love and trust and laughter, before you knew it, you were extending and expanding, one child, then another…and another.…

''Do your parents live in Hainesville, too?'' Randall asked.

''They live in Simcoe, a larger town about ten minutes down the road,'' Max replied, slightly uneasy. He hadn't told them about Randall coming to visit.

''It's great to hear about your family, because they're *my* family, too,'' Randall said shyly. ''I mean, Mom and Dad are my family, but their ancestors aren't. My dad traced the Tipton family tree right back to the Pilgrims, and my mom's family came from Hungary after the Second World War. It's interesting, but they're not part of me, not really.'' Randall lifted one shoulder in a deprecating gesture. ''Do you think I could meet your parents—my grandparents—sometime?''

Max wasn't sure his mother and father would agree to that. After all, they hadn't wanted Max to have anything to do with Randall when he was born. Although he wasn't about to tell Randall that, neither would he pretend to his parents the boy didn't exist.

For now, he avoided the question, saying, "I'm an only child, too. I know what it's like to want family. I'll call them soon."

They fell quiet for a while, listening to the lapping of the water against the pilings and the distant chug-chug of a generator. Max breathed in fresh salt air and the not-unpleasant odor of sun-warmed creosote on the pilings of the dock. With his son by his side, life was good.

Randall scratched at the dock with the point of Max's fishing knife. "If you'd married my mother I would have grown up here."

How could Max answer such a statement? How *should* he reply? He'd thought this one through any number of times in the past thirteen years and always came to the same conclusion. He and Lanni never would have lasted had they married. Despite a superficial attraction, they were too different and their marriage would likely have broken down. Odds were, she'd have been awarded custody of Randall and Max *still* wouldn't have a son living with him, although he would undoubtedly have seen more of him.

"I would have liked very much for you to have grown up with me," Max said, putting a hand on Randall's shoulder.

Randall glanced up, eyes bright, and Max's heart twisted as he forced himself to utter the bittersweet truth. "But it was better for you that you were adopted by the Tiptons and were raised in a stable home."

Randall's teeth bit down on his bottom lip and his gaze reached across the river. "I guess you're right."

Max could tell his son didn't believe it any more than he did.

CHAPTER EIGHT

FULL OF MISGIVINGS, Kelly let herself in the front door on Thursday evening. What on earth had she been thinking to agree to the dance lesson? Especially when Max hadn't even called, just sent her an e-mail asking her to pick him up!

It wasn't his signature, *your loving husband,* that had changed her mind, although she'd certainly felt a pang when she'd read it. Empty words in light of what he *hadn't* said, like apologize, or agree to counseling.

No, the reason she'd come was simple: she just plain missed him.

"Mommy!" Tammy called, spotting her as she entered the family room. "That's a pretty dress."

Tammy and Tina were sitting opposite Randall at the dining table, finger-painting. Bowls of water, trays of paints and colorful soggy paper littered the area around them. Whereas the little girls had paint all over their hands and faces, Randall had dipped the tip of one finger and was making careful impressionistic daubs on his paper.

"Do a handprint, Randall," Tina urged him. "Come on. It's fun." Randall shook his head.

"Tammy, honey," Kelly said, interrupting. "Where's your father?"

"I'm here." Max came into the room through the door from the garage, wiping his hands on grease-stained overalls. "Why are you all dressed up?"

Suddenly self-conscious of her low neckline and swirling skirt, Kelly retorted, "Why are you *not?*"

His gaze went from surprised to bewildered.

"Hello?" she said. "Latin dancing? Tonight is the first lesson."

He shook his head. "I didn't think you'd want to go."

"What? Then why did you e-mail—"

"I'll look after the kids if you want to go out," Randall broke in loudly.

Kelly frowned at the boy. "Excuse me. We're having a conversation here."

"I take care of the neighbor children when their mother goes shopping," Randall continued, undeterred. "They're about the same age as Tina and Tammy."

"Yay! Randy's going to baby-sit us," Tina yelled.

"Handprint, Randy. Do a handprint," Tammy chanted.

"Hang on," Max said, looking confused. "Randall, I thought you said you canceled the dance lessons."

"That's rather a lot to take upon yourself, isn't it?" Kelly demanded of the boy before he could answer. Until she'd received Max's e-mail, Kelly had more or less decided to do that herself, but Randall's intervention had her outraged.

"Ease up, Kel," Max said. "He only did it because he thought that was what I wanted."

This brought her up short. "Well...is it?"

His gaze traveled up her legs to her nipped-in waist, and higher, to her hint of cleavage. He seemed to make up his mind on the spot. "No. It's probably not too late to reinstate ourselves. Give me five minutes to clean up."

Kelly moved into the kitchen. "Go get ready. I'll fix the kids some dinner."

"We've all eaten," Randall informed her. Then, with a look of grim determination, he rolled up his sleeve and placed his whole hand in a plate of blue paint, to the great delight of Tammy and Tina.

Kelly glanced over the immaculate kitchen. The granite countertop was shining and even the sink was scrubbed out. "It doesn't look like it."

"Randall caught a four-pound sockeye." Max threw the boy a proud smile and exited the room.

"It was yummy." Tina rubbed her stomach with her paint-covered hand, making Kelly wince.

"We helped clean up after," Tammy added.

So. He was taking over her jobs around the house, too. "You girls helped? My, my. Randall, you must be some kind of miracle worker."

Although her words were praise, her tone oozed sarcasm. Randall had been grinning foolishly at his handprint. Now his cheeks turned bright red, clashing unbecomingly with his hair. Kelly felt ashamed and bit her tongue before she could say anything else unkind. To ride him wasn't fair. But she couldn't help resenting the hell out of the fact he was here in her home and she was not. Or that he was ingratiating himself with her children while she was missing them badly.

"Where are Beth and Robyn?" she asked.

"Beth's at a friend's house and Robyn's in her room," Randall said. "Beth's room, I mean."

Leaving the children to their paints, Kelly went along to see Robyn. She tapped on the door and waited.

"Who is it?" Robyn asked, her voice faintly belligerent.

"It's me." Kelly pushed open the door and found

Robyn lying on the top bunk, reading. "Who did you think it was?"

"That awful Randall," Robyn said, making a face. "He's always asking me if I want to use his computer or something stupid like that." She put down her book. "You look nice. Are you and Daddy going out?"

"Latin-dance lessons."

Robyn brightened. "That's good."

"We planned this before Randall," Kelly said with a shrug, and sat in the desk chair. From now on, her life would be divided into Before Randall and After Randall. "You don't like him much, do you?"

"Why should I?" Robyn said bitterly. "If he wasn't here, you wouldn't have left home."

Kelly didn't bother trotting out the fiction that she was away because she was taking care of Gran. "Randall's important to your father," she said. "He'll leave eventually."

"Then will you come home so everything can go back to normal?" Robyn's eyes pleaded with her to say yes.

Kelly rose and leaned on the bunk bed to stroke her daughter's arm. "I don't know, sweetheart," she whispered. "But, Robyn, no matter what happens with your dad and me, none of it's your fault. We both love you and always will."

Robyn bit her bottom lip and nodded, tears forming in her eyes.

Kelly brushed dark bangs out of Robyn's eyes. "You need a haircut. I'll make an appointment for you, okay? We could go out for lunch afterward."

"Sure, Mom." Robyn forced a wavering smile. "That sounds great. Can I get streaks this time?"

Max appeared in the doorway, dressed in chinos and a light blue polo shirt that mirrored the color of his eyes. "Kelly, are you ready?"

Kelly kissed Robyn on the cheek. "No streaks. See you soon. I love you, honey."

She walked toward Max, conscious of his gaze, conscious of how good he looked. He didn't shift to give her room as she moved past him through the doorway. Her shoulder brushed his chest; her hip touched his thigh.

"You look nice." His voice was a low thrum in her ear.

Anticipation buzzed through her veins. "So do you."

At the car, he held the door for her, waiting to shut it while she adjusted her skirt. Only when he'd turned out of the driveway onto River Road did she realize *he* was driving *her* car. She thought about protesting, then decided that after driving around all day showing properties, she didn't mind sitting back and relaxing for a change.

"Feel like some music?"

She nodded and he tuned the radio to easy listening.

Just as though they were on a date. Tonight just might be fun.

"Do you remember our first date—the junior prom?"

His grin came quick. "Will you ever let me forget?"

She chuckled softly. "You rang the doorbell and barely said hello before you threw up on my new shoes."

"I had the flu."

"Gramps thought you'd been drinking. He almost made me stay home."

"But you insisted I wasn't that kind of guy."

"We had a great time that night, didn't we?"

Smiling, Max nodded. They were replaying dialogue they'd perfected over the years. Somehow it eased the awkwardness of the present situation.

Kelly settled back in her seat as they passed through farmland glowing pink and blue in the twilight. "Max, there's something I don't understand. If you knew Randall canceled the lessons, why did you e-mail me about going tonight?"

He took his gaze off the road briefly. "I didn't e-mail you."

"Yes, you did." She turned in her seat to stare at him. "You asked me to drive because your car was broken."

Max brought the station wagon to a halt at a four-way stop and twisted in his seat. "There's nothing wrong with my car."

She frowned. "You were working on it when I got to the house."

"I was changing the oil."

"Is that all? Then why did you e-mail me?"

"I didn't."

"Then who did? *Someone* signed your name."

With a puzzled shake of his head, Max started through the intersection. "Robyn must have done it. She's upset about you being away. But she knows she's not allowed on my computer. I'll have to speak to her."

Kelly leaned back in her seat; Max was probably right. "Leave her alone. She's upset about Randall."

"Randall was only trying to help when he canceled the lessons."

"Oh, he's helping, all right." Max started to speak and she waved him to silence. "Don't bother defending him. We're going to get there and find our names crossed off the list."

One hand draped over the wheel, Max shrugged. "You worry too much."

But Kelly *was* worried. She was counting on these dance lessons as an excuse to spend time with Max. Seeing him last weekend had brought home to her how much she missed him. Holding his hand reminded her of those small intimacies she'd given up by leaving him: the casual touch, the warm glance, the shared smile that needed no words for understanding. She felt as if she'd lost her best friend.

The dance studio was located above the Simcoe billiard hall. Max and Kelly climbed the long narrow flight of stairs to find nine or ten other couples already grouped around the room.

One of the instructors, a thirty-something man in black pants and a white shirt open to midchest, stood near the door with a clipboard. He listened to Kelly's slightly garbled tale of their mistaken cancellation, and said, "No problem. The class wasn't full, anyway. Your names?" he added, pen poised to write them down.

"Kelly and Max Walker." She peered over his shoulder at his list of participants. "Hey, there we are." She glanced at Max. "Now I'm really confused."

"Forget it," Max said over the sudden sound of

Latin rhythms coming from a portable stereo system. "I think we're about to begin."

The man in the white shirt left them to join his partner at the front of the room. They introduced themselves as Luís and Esmerelda before stepping onto the dance floor. With their gazes locked and their movements exaggerated for their pupils' benefit, the sultry pair demonstrated the tango.

"They make it look so easy," Kelly whispered to Max.

"Ah, it's a snap. Come here." He pulled her into his arms.

Heads butted together, they gazed at their feet and concentrated, occasionally glancing at the instructors for illumination. Kelly giggled as they stumbled over each other and bumped into other dancers. "We'll never get it."

"Sure we will." Max dipped her backward without warning. "I'm a natural. *Eet's* my Latin blood."

"Max!" she squealed. "My very American blood is rushing to my head. And my boobs are falling out of my dress. Max!"

"Call me Rickee." He hauled her back up to lock his hips with hers in a sensual back-and-forth movement.

An erotic thrill ran through her despite her laughter. Max had no more idea how to tango than she did, but he could make her heart beat faster. "Ouch!" she cried as he trod on her foot. "What was I thinking when I bought these lessons?"

"You were theenking about being in my arms," he said with a leer, impersonating Ricky Martin. Or was it Ricky Ricardo?

Her eyes met his and their laughter faded. Tension thickened the air between them. He'd hit close to the bone and somehow he knew it. How could she deny the truth when her flushed cheeks and ardent gaze gave her away? Deliberately she moved apart from him. No matter what her feelings she mustn't lose sight of the fact that nothing was resolved between them.

"No, no, no." Esmerelda swooped down on them, a vision in scarlet and black. "You are much too far apart. The tango is a sensual dance." She gyrated briefly to illustrate, while Kelly exchanged an amused glance with Max. Then Esmerelda put one hand on Kelly's back and one hand on Max's and pushed until they were plastered together the length of their torsos. "That's better. Now, move with each other. Listen to the music and the feet will take care of themselves."

"Yeah, right," Kelly muttered, too focused on the sensation of Max moving against her to even hear the music, much less worry about what her feet were doing. Too conscious of his hand in the small of her back, pressing her ever closer; of his breath whispering like a warm breeze across the top of her head and the spicy scent of his soap mingling with the sweat of exertion.

He dipped his head to murmur, ''Did I mention how extremely sexy you look in that dress?''

She tipped her head back to answer but found her mind at a loss and her throat too dry to speak. She knew how he wanted the evening to end. She wanted that, too, but not as much as she wanted to him to acknowledge the validity of her feelings about Randall.

Later, as they drove home in silence, Max reached for her hand where it lay on her thigh. Flustered, she pulled it away to lift her hair off her still-damp neck. ''That was fun,'' she said with a little smile. ''I'm glad we went.''

''Me, too.'' He withdrew his hand. ''How's work going?''

''Good. I have some clients who are seriously interested in the Harper house.''

His eyebrows lifted in surprise. ''You actually found a sucker who would even look at the place?''

She slapped his hand, perversely seeking contact now that he'd withdrawn it. ''It's a beautiful house. It just needs a little TLC. The interested couple are a carpenter and his wife who want to turn it into a B and B.''

''It's a wonderful old house,'' Max admitted. ''I'd buy it myself if I had the money and time to fix it up. Did you fib about the roof the way Ray wanted you to?''

''What do you think?''

One side of his mouth kicked up in an indulgent smile. ''I think you're the most honest real estate agent this side of the Rockies.''

Kelly smiled radiantly at him. ''Thank you.''

A few minutes later he pulled into their driveway. Before she could get out to go around to the driver's seat, Max curled his fingers around the back of her neck and pressed his mouth down on hers, familiar and so achingly sweet she could scarcely breathe.

''Call your grandmother and tell her you're sleeping at home tonight,'' he murmured against her lips.

''But—''

''Ruth will be okay till morning.''

Kelly wasn't worried about Gran; she was worried about herself. If she gave in, even for one night, she would have lost the entire battle. ''I can't. Until we sort out our problems, until you apologize and agree to counseling, we're not getting back together. And there will be no sex.''

''That's blackmail.''

"It's how I feel. You use sex to patch things up, but I can't make love unless we're emotionally on an even keel."

Max snorted. "You can't tell me you weren't thinking about sex when we were on the dance floor."

"Are you *ever* going to apologize?"

"I never meant to hurt you, Kelly—you know that. I have nothing to apologize for."

Kelly faced front so she didn't have to look at him. "You are so stubborn."

"What about you?" Max propped one arm on the steering wheel as he leaned toward her. "You refuse to acknowledge the importance of my son in my life."

She flashed him a glance full of hurt. "You've got a family—me and the girls."

His gaze dropped to her breasts, visible above the low scooped neckline. "If you weren't trying to turn me on, why did you wear that dress?"

Ooh, she hated it when he did that. "Okay. Yes, I wanted to be attractive to you. But I wasn't thinking about sex—at least not right away. I was hoping we could relax in each other's company enough to talk."

"Talk?" He drew back in disbelief. "Lady, you've got some weird way of starting a conversation."

She crossed her arms across her chest. "I'm still waiting for an apology."

"We're going around in circles. Fine." He threw up his hands. "I'm sorry you got hurt. Is that better?"

"No," she said, hurt afresh by his hard tone of voice. "You should be saying, 'I'm sorry I hurt you.' It's all about admitting responsibility for your actions."

"Don't put words into my mouth. Why should I bother saying anything when you say it for me?"

"I have to say it for you because you never admit when you've done something wrong!" she cried, exasperated. "If you would only say you're sorry and mean it, I might be able to forget and move on. Or at least talk through it."

"You're getting hung up on one little aspect of what happened," Max complained. "Randall isn't even the issue. You know what the problem is between us? We'd planned from the beginning to have at least five children and you've reneged on the deal."

"I'm not going to sit here and listen to this." She grabbed her purse, yanked open the car door and stomped around to the other side. This was so stupid. *Max* was so stupid. "Get out so I can go home."

Max slowly unfolded his long body from the car

and placed the keys in her open palm. With a for-giving smile he dropped a kiss on her forehead. "Next week, I'll pick you up."

Stunned, she closed her hand around the keys. After all that he still wanted to go dancing? Kelly felt as though she'd been bludgeoned with a copy of *Men Are From Mars, Women Are From Venus.*

Yet, at the moment, the dance lessons were the only link they had besides the children.

Sighing, she said, "Okay. See you next week."

Max lingered. "Not until then? Won't you be coming around—"

"To make dinner and do the laundry? Of course I will."

"You know that's not why I want you home, Kel. You belong here. The girls need you." He started to put his arms around her. "How about we end this date the way we ended our first? With a kiss."

Sidestepping him, she held up a hand. "Let's just say good-night while our tempers are intact."

Kelly got back in her car and drove away. In the rearview mirror Max's silhouette stood out blackly against the security light, as hip cocked, arms akimbo, he watched her leave. She sighed. If only they *could* go back to the innocence of their courting days.

THE NEXT DAY RANDALL WAS in his room, playing chess on the computer, when he heard the front door open. Max had just left for Seattle and a meeting with clients. Beth and the twins were in the backyard, having a game of scrub softball, and Robyn had locked herself in Beth's room, with a book. Randall got up to see who was at the door. The Walkers were great people, but they were pretty lax about things like locking doors. Anybody could just walk in.

When he saw Kelly, arms laden with grocery bags, he halted midway down the hall. He'd never had to deal with her on her own before and now he glanced around, hoping that by some miracle, the twins or Beth would come running. Even the dogs would provide a welcome distraction. But they were out back with the younger girls. Robyn, he hoped, *wouldn't* appear.

"Uh, hi, Mrs. Walker." He made himself move forward, reaching for the grocery bag balanced precariously on top of the two in her arms. "Let me help."

Only the fact that the bag was about to fall produced her muffled "Thanks"; he was sure of that. He would have taken one of the other bags, as well, but she surged ahead, leaving him to follow in her wake.

"Any more groceries in the car?" he asked as he deposited the bag on the island benchtop.

"No, that's it. Thanks." Without casting him a second glance, she began stowing milk and butter in the fridge.

Randall handed her a carton of eggs. "Did you enjoy the dancing?"

"It was fine." Kelly stepped around him to reach for the bags of vegetables and fruit and headed back to the refrigerator.

Randall opened the door for her. "Were there lots of people?"

"Enough." Kelly backed away from the fridge. "You can close the door now. The cold air is getting out."

Flushing, Randall pushed it shut. He wanted to get on her good side, but she wasn't making it easy for him. Plus he truly wanted to know how their evening had gone. Max had been grumpy and uncommunicative this morning. Randall retreated to the island bench and started folding the paper bags along their creases. He'd noticed the clean empty jars and yogurt containers in one of the cupboards and deduced Kelly didn't like throwing things away.

Kelly straightened from putting the last of the fresh produce in the crisper, leaving out a selection of vegetables. He handed her the folded bags.

She did a double take and met his gaze for the first time since she'd arrived. "Thanks."

"Beth showed me your plant room," he said as Kelly got out the chopping board and started slicing onions. "The flower arrangements are really pretty." She merely nodded, so he continued, "Afterward I looked up dried flowers on the Internet. People sell stuff just like yours by e-mail."

"Is that so?"

He thought he detected a flicker of interest, but she didn't ask him about the Web sites so he let the matter drop. "Can I give you a hand with anything? I usually help Mom with dinner. Dad had a section of the kitchen counter lowered for her, but she still finds cooking awkward."

Kelly gave him a tight, closemouthed smile. "You're a real helpful guy, aren't you, Randall?"

"Uh, yeah, I guess," he said uncertainly. "So...?"

"So why don't you find something else to do?" There was an underlying tinge of what almost sounded like desperation to her voice. "If I need help I'll call Robyn or Beth."

"Sure." Completely crushed, he backed away.

He would have gone straight to his room, but Tina burst through the sliding door. "Randy, we need you.

Someone has to play catcher 'cuz Tammy keeps ducking when I'm up to bat.''

Up till now he'd avoided all their efforts to get him to play softball, but at the moment it looked like a pretty good option. At least *someone* wanted him around. ''Okay.''

Tina took him by the hand and dragged him to the makeshift diamond in the backyard. Beth tossed him a baseball mitt. The leather felt stiff and the mitt was too small, but he jammed his fingers in anyway and tentatively punched a fist into the cavity where the ball would—theoretically, at least—land.

''Stand behind Tina,'' Beth instructed him from the piece of weathered board that served as a pitcher's mound.

Randall got into position, awkwardly holding his mitt out to the side at what he imagined was the correct angle.

''No, no, no.'' Tammy, a diminutive expert, strode over, blond curls bouncing, and nudged him out of the way. ''You crouch down, like this,'' she said, demonstrating. ''And hold your mitt up, like this.''

Randall crouched and stuck up his arm in the required manner. Beth wound up her arm dramatically and pitched the ball. Tina swung wildly and Randall shut his eyes. The ball missed the bat and went over his shoulder and into the lilac bushes.

"Never mind," Beth said cheerfully. "We'll try again."

On the second pitch, Tina connected and the ball rolled toward shortstop. Beth scooped up the ball and threw it to Tammy on first base. Tammy missed and Tina kept going around the bases. Tammy got the ball and tossed it back to Beth, who threw it to Randall just as Tina touched third.

"Go, Tina!" Randall cheered her on, oblivious to his duties as catcher. "Come on, you can make it."

"Catch the ball, Randy!" Beth yelled.

The ball bounced on the dirt patch that was home plate and disappeared into the lilacs.

"Randy!" Beth threw up her hands as Tina ran home. "You're supposed to catch the ball and tag her out."

"Oh! Sorry." Mortified, he plunged into the bushes after the errant ball, emerging a moment later with his glasses cockeyed and leaves in his hair.

One of the leaves fell into the gap behind his glasses, obscuring his vision and blocking his eye like a pirate patch. Tina began to laugh, then Tammy. Then Beth.

"You should see your face," Beth said between giggles. "You look like you're going to explode."

Their girlish chortles, restrained at first, gained in volume until the air was filled with uproarious merriment. Randall felt his face turn a deeper shade of red. Oh, man, this was worse than when that creep Kevin Turnbull had teased him because he couldn't kick a football. Randall dropped the ball on home plate and started to slink off.

"Hey, Randy, where are you going?" Tammy called. A small hand pulled on his shirt and he glanced down to see the little girl smiling up at him. "We're not laughing *at* you—we're laughing *with* you. Mom says we always have to make sure people know that," she added parenthetically.

"Yeah," piped up Tina. "You looked so cute when you were cheering Tammy home. Kinda dumb, but cute."

Cute? A four-year-old was calling him cute? Randall couldn't help but smile. Encouraged, the twins danced around his legs, hooting with mirth. Randall shook his head at their antics. His grin widened and moments later he was laughing, too, laughing for the sake of laughing until his sides hurt.

"Okay, okay." He held up his hands to stem their giggles. "Are you going to teach me how to play softball, or what?"

By the time Kelly called them into dinner, Randall had grass stains on the knees of his chinos and his legs ached from the unaccustomed exercise. He washed his hands at the bathroom sink and watched the dirt swirl down the drain. What would his mom think if she could see him now? He hoped she would simply be glad he was having fun.

He took his place at the dinner table between Beth and Tammy as Kelly set out big bowls of flat noodles and beef stroganoff. The savory aroma hit his nostrils and set off a loud rumble in his stomach. From across the table Robyn gave him a disgusted look that made Randall's cheeks burn.

"Someone's hungry," Max said, grinning. "Dig in."

After dinner was over and the dishes cleared away, Kelly disappeared into her plant room, and Beth and the twins went out to feed the chickens. Randall stayed behind in the kitchen to dry the pots and put them away. Kelly had told him to let them dry in the rack, but Audrey had taught him to leave the kitchen spotless.

Robyn was about to wander off, too, when her father stopped her. "Robyn, I want to talk to you."

Randall didn't know what Miss Perfect could have done to warrant that stern voice from Max, but he thought he'd better leave them alone.

Before he could, Max said, "You know I don't like you girls playing around on my computer."

Randall froze, dish towel in hand. Max and Robyn seemed to have forgotten he was there and now he couldn't have walked out of that room if his life had depended on it.

Robyn stared at her father. "I know that. I haven't been near your computer."

"Robyn." Max's voice held reproof and was patently disbelieving. "Someone e-mailed your mother, pretending to be me. Just admit it and I won't be angry."

"Honest, Dad, I haven't touched your e-mail." She was beginning to get upset.

He passed a hand through his hair and his voice softened slightly. "Robyn, I know this...situation has been difficult for you, but your mother and I will work out our problems. We don't need 'help' that will only complicate and confuse the issues."

"I swear to you I haven't touched your e-mail."

"Then who did?"

Randall spoke up. "Me."

CHAPTER NINE

MAX AND ROBYN TURNED to stare at him. Randall felt the heat creep up his neck and knew a deep agony of regret as Max's face registered shock and disappointment.

"I'm sorry," he mumbled. "I never thought..." He hadn't expected to get caught, and he so rarely did anything wrong that he hadn't considered the consequences, much less someone else getting blamed for his actions.

"Robyn," Max said, still staring at Randall, "please leave us."

Robyn walked slowly out of the room, casting puzzled glances over her shoulder.

"Come here, Randall," Max said, moving to the family room. "Sit down."

Twisting the dish towel between his hands, Randall went and sat on the far end of the couch from Max.

"Why did you do it?" Max asked.

Randall shrugged. Max's steady gaze tied his tongue.

"Never mind. I think I know. But, Randall, you're a smart kid. You must have realized it was wrong. I wouldn't have expected this of you."

"I'm sorry," Randall said in a low voice, looking at the floor. God, he hoped Max wouldn't send him away. "I won't do it again."

"I believe you." Max was silent for a long moment. "As much as I deplore the sneakiness of your actions, I admire the fact that you wouldn't let Robyn take the blame."

Randall felt a trickle of relief; Max didn't hate him. "She had nothing to do with it, honest."

"I know. Do you remember what I told you the other day—that you shouldn't feel guilty about Kelly and me?"

Randall hitched one shoulder higher than the other and risked a glance at Max. "It's hard not to. Robyn hates me because her mom's not home."

"The situation isn't your fault," Max insisted. "You've got to trust me on this."

Randall nodded, even though he knew that while Max might not blame him, Max's wife and daughter certainly did.

"Don't worry about Robyn and Kelly," Max said,

as if he knew what Randall was thinking. "I'll have a talk with them—"

"No, please don't," Randall said quickly. "That'll only make things worse."

Max considered a moment, then nodded. "Maybe you're right. They'll come around eventually. Now, don't you have something better to do than polish pots and pans?"

Randall grinned and folded the dish towel. "My computer chess tournament. I'm into the finals."

Half an hour later, he was frowning at the computer screen, calculating his crucial next move, when he heard a knock at the half-closed door. "Just a second, please," he called. If he moved the queen's pawn, he put his knight in jeopardy. If he didn't, he would surely lose his bishop.

The knock came again. "Are you busy?" a voice asked.

Robyn! Surprise threw off his concentration. Randall spun his chair around. Robyn never spoke to him unless absolutely necessary and then only in monosyllables. Which was okay, but he wished she liked him a little.

"I was just playing chess," he said. "Come in."

She stepped inside the room and, after a slight hesitation, shut the door. Weirder and weirder. He felt awkward inviting her to sit down in her own room, but he gestured to the bed. And promptly felt himself turn brickred.

"You've really got to work on that blushing problem, you realize." She moved aside his computer magazines and sat primly on the bed with her legs pressed together and her hands tucked under her knees.

"If I knew how to stop it, I would," he muttered, then added ungraciously, "what do you want?"

"To thank you for telling Dad it was you and not me who used his e-mail."

"Well, of course." Letting someone else take the blame for something he'd done would never occur to him.

"Why did you do it?" Robyn went on. "E-mail my mom and pretend you were my dad. Was it to trick her into coming over for the dance lessons?"

Randall nodded. "I feel bad that she left because of me. I wanted to bring her and Max back together."

Robyn seemed satisfied with his answer. "It worked. They went out. Your e-mail stunt gave me an idea. Will you help me try something else?"

"What exactly do you mean?" he asked warily. "I promised Max I wouldn't interfere anymore."

Robyn waved a graceful hand. "Dad will never

find out. And this time, if he does, I'll take the blame.''

She could be setting him up. She could be on the level. With Robyn, he just couldn't tell. She wasn't like Beth, open and straightforward.

''If you really want to make Dad happy you'll help me get Mom back,'' Robyn added persuasively.

In the end, Randall went with his gut feeling. If Robyn was so desperate to have her mother back that she would trust him, that should mean he could trust her. And he wanted Max happy. Surely in this case, the ends justified the means.

''Okay,'' he said at last. ''What's your plan?''

THAT SATURDAY MORNING Max exited the florist's shop, pleased with himself. Why hadn't he thought of flowers earlier? Kelly had liked her anniversary roses. The huge bouquet of Kelly's favorite blooms he'd arranged to be delivered to her office was sure to be a hit.

Strolling back down Main Street, he encountered elderly Mrs. Thompson, and an excess of high spirits caused him to inquire after her health. As she launched into a detailed reply on her favorite subject Max shifted his feet and began to regret his impulse. She was a dear, but she did carry on and he had to get back to work.

He was half listening to Mrs. Thompson recount her bunion operation, when he spotted something that jerked him fully alert. Robyn and Randall were walking toward him—together. Robyn and Randall? Those two couldn't be in the same room without Robyn making some snide comment, and whenever the boy could, he avoided her. What had caused them to seek each other's company?

Robyn and Randall noticed Max two seconds after he saw them and halted abruptly. They looked at each other in alarm and darted into the adjacent drugstore.

"Excuse me, Mrs. Thompson," Max said, edging away. "I just saw my daughter go into Blackwell's and I have to speak to her."

"All right, Max. Lovely to see you again. You and Kelly come over for coffee and doughnuts sometime."

"Thanks, we'll do that." And he was off.

He found the pair skulking along the far wall, leafing through magazines.

"Hi, kids." He slowed to a nonchalant stroll. "What's happening?"

"Oh, hi, Dad," Robyn replied, innocent as a newborn.

Randall lifted his gaze from the pages of *Computer Time* to reveal an expression saturated with guilt.

"What are you two up to?" Max casually posed his question to Robyn. "Did you entice Randall on a shopping expedition?"

"I'm just…showing him the town," Robyn replied. "All Beth ever does with him is play softball or throw the Frisbee around."

"I see. Enjoying the tour, Randall?"

Randall nodded, avoiding eye contact.

"So, what's your next stop?" Max asked. "The library?"

"Uh, I'm not sure," Robyn said. "Maybe the Burger Shack. Shouldn't you be working, Dad?"

"I had some errands in town." He wasn't going to get any more out of these two. "Want a ride home later?"

"No, that's okay. We'll walk or take the bus."

"I'll see you around, then."

"Bye, Dad," Robyn said with obvious relief.

Randall muttered goodbye, too, and Max left. Whatever they were up to, it was obviously a secret. But they were both good kids so it couldn't be too bad. Could it?

"BOY, WAS THAT CLOSE." Randall watched Max walk away, his heart still beating fast. "I have a bad feeling about this. Maybe we should forget about your plan."

"Don't worry so much. Wait here." She ran to the drugstore exit, glanced down the street, then waved the all clear. Randall put his magazine back on the rack and made his way through the aisles. She grabbed his sleeve and tugged him in the direction of the florist's. "Come on. I saw Dad get into his car and drive off. He'll never know what we're up to."

Robyn chose the biggest bouquet they could afford with their pooled savings while Randall kept a lookout by the window, nervously glancing up and down the street.

"Come and sign the card," Robyn called. "Your handwriting is more masculine than mine. Anyway, Mom would recognize mine in an instant, even if I tried to disguise it. You know Dad's style. Try to copy it."

Randall balked. "I'm not signing Max's name. That would really be dishonest. Besides, I did that once and got in trouble."

"Then how's she going to know the flowers are from him?"

"Who else would send them?"

"You've got a point. Okay, sign it, *With love and devotion from your Not-So-Secret Admirer.*"

"Isn't that a bit sappy?" Randall said.

"It's beautiful." She shoved the pen in his hand. "Trust me. She'll love it."

LATER THAT MORNING, Kelly was humming as she put together the contract for the most satisfying sale of her career to date. A tiny voice niggled that it was one of the *only* satisfying sales, but she ignored it. Vindication was sweet.

She heard the bell over the door tinkle and paid no attention. Annette had gone to lunch, but Ray was out front.

A moment later, he came around the corner of her cubicle carrying the biggest bouquet of flowers she'd ever seen. "These are for you."

"Uh, thank you, Ray." Kelly felt sick at the thought of Ray giving her flowers.

"They're not from *me*." Ray seemed equally appalled at the thought that he would shell out for a huge bunch of flowers. The doorbell tinkled again. He thrust the flowers at her and left.

Kelly buried her face in the magnificent arrangement, breathing in the mingled perfumes of her favorite blooms. Drawing back, she opened the small square envelope tucked among the greenery. Familiar handwriting in architect's script read, *Just because I love you... Max.*

Kelly sank back in her chair, her heart swelling

with love. Oh, Max. So extravagant. What a romantic!

"You're not going to believe this!" Ray griped, coming around the corner with yet another bouquet of flowers.

Kelly stared in stunned surprise. "Don't tell me those are mine, too?" She swept aside her daily planner and the Woolridge contract to make room for the second huge display.

"According to the delivery boy, they are. Is it your birthday?"

Kelly shook her head. "These are from Max," she said, indicating the first bouquet. She tore open the second envelope and brought her head up. "A *Not-So Secret Admirer?*"

"And you're not even officially separated." Ray cast her a sly glance. "Are you seeing someone else?"

"No!" Kelly had told Ray she'd moved into the house on Linden Street to take care of her Gran, but she knew gossip around town hinted at trouble between her and Max. "I haven't a clue who would send these."

She peered closer at the card and her eyes narrowed. "The handwriting is awfully similar to Max's, although he's obviously tried to disguise it."

She passed the two cards to Ray. "What do you think?"

"You're right," he said after studying them. "They've got the same look about them, like hand-printed italics." He passed the cards back to Kelly. "But why would he send *two* bouquets? And why would he send the second one anonymously?"

"He sent two to be lavish, thinking I'll be doubly delighted," Kelly said slowly, her mind familiar with the workings of Max's. "And he didn't sign the second card because—" her mouth flattened into a grim line "—he knows I'd kill him for throwing away so much money on flowers when we can't afford it."

MAX HEARD THE FRONT DOOR open followed by the pounding of small feet as Tina and Tammy thundered past his office. They'd been at a birthday party all afternoon and Kelly had picked them up on her way home.

He found Kelly and the twins in the family room and was immediately accosted by four-year-olds hyped on candy and birthday cake.

"Daddy, Daddy." Tina raced toward him and connected so hard she almost knocked him over. "I won Pin the Tail on the Donkey."

Tammy tugged on his pant leg. "And I won the

egg-and-spoon race.'' She dug in her treat bag and pulled out a squashy caramel. ''Want a candy?''

''No, thanks.'' He gave the girls both a hug, but his gaze was on Kelly.

She was smiling as if all *her* birthdays had come at once, and his own mouth lifted in a grin as smug as the Cheshire cat's. Those flowers had really done the trick. He'd thought she might bring them home with her, but maybe she preferred that they brighten up her office.

''Listen to this, Daddy,'' Tammy shouted, blowing a noisemaker in his ear.

''Take that outside, please, honey,'' he said. ''In fact, why don't you two put on your bathing suits and run under the sprinkler.''

''Come on, Tina. The sprinkler!'' Tammy yelled, and the girls tore off to their room.

As Kelly brushed past, he leaned in close to smell her hair. ''You look as though you had a good day.''

Her smile widened and her eyes danced. ''I had a *fabulous* day. An ultrastupendous, unbeatable day of all days!''

''Yeah?'' He grinned. ''Go on. What happened?''

Exultant, she raised two fists in the air. ''I sold the Harper house!''

''You're wel— *What?*'' It was so *not* what he was

expecting to hear he could only stand and gape, awash in disappointment.

"Yes! Victory at last is mine. And you should have seen the look on Ray's face when the price I negotiated was five thousand dollars more than he'd expected."

Despite his disappointment, Max was impressed. "Who bought it—the bed-and-breakfast people?"

"Uh-huh. Hal Woolridge would have spotted the problems, anyway, but he thanked me for being so honest. Even better, he made a point of telling Ray how pleased they were with my service." She cha-cha'd over to the fridge. "Have we got any wine? I feel like celebrating."

"There's a bottle of chardonnay in there." Max got a couple of glasses from the cabinet and set them on the counter next to where she was opening the bottle with a corkscrew. Unable to help himself, he reached out and sifted his fingers through her shiny, silky hair. "Anything else happen of note?"

She flicked her hair back as if his hand were an annoying insect. "No, I don't think so...."

"Nothing? Not one little thing?"

Her face remained blank.

"Flowers?"

"Oh...the *flowers!*" To his surprise, her smile

faded. "Max, I appreciate the gesture. It was *so* sweet. But honestly, did you have to get so many?"

"But...I thought you'd like them. You love flowers."

"I do. They're beautiful. But they must have cost a fortune." Kelly snatched up the sheaf of bills sitting on the counter and thrust them under his nose. "Look at these...gas, electricity, telephone. And our grocery bill has skyrocketed since a certain teenage boy joined the household."

"Oh, for God's sake!" Max pushed aside the bills and walked away, leaving his wine untouched. "Congratulations on selling the Harper house," he said sarcastically from the doorway. "Maybe with your commission we'll be able to afford to eat for another month." With that parting shot he stalked down the hall toward his office.

"Flowers and chocolates aren't the way to a woman's heart," Kelly yelled after him.

Max paused in the hall, waiting for her to inform him what *was* the key to her heart. But the next instant he heard the CD player go on and knew he would not receive enlightenment tonight.

"WOMEN!" Max expostulated to Ben and Nick the following week when he found them playing one-on-one at the high school basketball court. They, like him, had come early to practice before the game. "Can't live with them. Can't shoot 'em."

Nick chuckled and passed the ball across the court to him. "Trouble in paradise?"

Max dribbled to the hoop and made the toss. The ball bounced off the backboard and into Ben's waiting hands.

"Uh-oh," Ben said, glancing at Nick. "Max never misses a shot. He must be having another bad day."

"Want to talk about it, buddy?" Nick wiped his damp face with the hem of his T-shirt.

Max threw up his hands. "Chocolates didn't work. Flowers didn't work. What do I do now?"

"Sex?" Ben suggested. "Whenever Geena and I spar, a trip to the bedroom usually smoothes over the rough edges."

"In my experience, you've got to soften 'em up first," Nick countered. "A little cuddling, a few compliments, then before you know it, they've forgotten there was even a problem."

Max shook his head. "The chocolate and flowers were supposed to soften her up, and as for sex, forget it! I'm not even allowed to touch her hair. She *says* all she wants is for me to apologize, but I know that what she really wants is for me to disown Randall." He shoved a hand through his hair, leaving it ruffled. "I can't do that."

"And you shouldn't have to, buddy," Nick said, slapping him on the back.

"Maybe it's time to stop softening her up and start playing hardball," Ben said.

Max stared at him. "What do you mean?"

"Forget about tackling this logically and start looking at the problem like a woman—emotionally." Ben tucked the basketball under his arm. "Kelly has to be feeling left out. After all, she's at Ruth's and the rest of you, including Randall, are having a great ol' time in her home. She's on the outside, looking in."

"I know," Max said. "It's bad."

"No, it's *good,*" said Nick, who apparently saw where Ben was going with this. "You've got to use her fear of being left out to bring her back into the fold. Right, Ben?"

"Exactly," Ben said approvingly. "What you do is, you have a party, a barbecue or something, to introduce the rest of us to Randall. Then when she sees how great it is to be together with the whole family and how everyone takes to the boy, she'll start to think, 'Hey, maybe *I'm* wrong.'"

"I dunno." Max scratched his head. "Right or wrong, Kelly's got this thing about having her feelings 'validated.' Trouble is, if *everything's* about *feelings,* and all the important stuff is, then *she's* always right.''

Nick chuckled. "Face it, buddy, when it comes to rationalizing their way to being right, women have us beat hands down."

"Still, a party might not be a bad idea," Max said thoughtfully. "Kelly loves parties. Plus Randall would love to meet everyone—he's very interested in his roots—and I know you'd all like him."

"'Course we would," Ben said. "Just tell us when and we'll be there."

"Maybe we should wait until Ruth is up and around," Max said.

"She's been off her crutches for over a week," Ben said, surprise coloring his voice. "Didn't you know?"

"No." Max's mouth set in a grim line. "Kelly is still staying over there nights."

"Hey, fellas," Mitchell, a member of the Simcoe team, called as he jogged onto court. "What ya doing standing around? Let's play."

"This week we're going to whup your asses," Max called jovially. To Nick and Ben he said, "I'll organize the barbecue for next Sunday. But one thing's for sure, I'm not going to humiliate myself again. If she wants to come home, *she's* going to have to ask *me* to take her back."

"THIS WAS A GREAT IDEA, getting everyone together for a barbecue, Kel," Erin said, returning to the kitchen after putting Erik down for a nap in the living room. "You should have let us bring something, though. You've got a lot of mouths to feed."

"Oh, it's no trouble." Kelly was busy threading cubes of marinated chicken onto wooden skewers. She'd been up early making the salads, which sat wrapped in plastic and ready to go on the table. Once she'd finished the chicken she just had to do the hamburger patties.... "The barbecue wasn't exactly my idea. Max came home from his basketball game last week and informed me he'd arranged the whole thing with Nick and Ben. Not that I mind," she added. "I'm always glad to get together with my family."

But she and Max used to plan social occasions together and his going ahead without her only served as another reminder of how far they'd drifted apart. In fact, he'd treated her so much as an outsider she'd had to insist on being allowed to organize the food.

"Well, I for one am glad to finally meet Randall," Geena said. She had ignored Kelly's refusal to accept help and was adding fresh strawberries and light rum to the ice and sugar syrup in the blender. "He's a real sweetheart."

"He's very considerate," Erin agreed.

"And so patient with the twins," Gran chimed in

from the dining table. She'd found the bag of hot-dog buns and was busy slicing them.

That was the whole trouble with Randall, Kelly thought irritably; to find fault with him was almost impossible. Even Robyn had made friends with the boy, as the astonishing conversation Kelly had over-heard between the pair that morning testified. Which reminded her, she owed Max an apology.

"Don't bother with the buns, Gran," Kelly said. "I'll get them in a minute."

"Whether it was your idea or not, putting on a barbecue for Randall is a kind gesture," Gran told her, obstinately continuing to slice. "Whatever your issues with Max, I'm glad to know you've tried to make Randall feel welcome."

Guilt stabbed Kelly, just as she jabbed her thumb with the pointed end of the skewer. She hadn't been as nice to Randall as she could have been, but while she hated to think she'd made any child feel un-wanted, she couldn't help resenting him. The truth was, today was only worsening matters. Her family had taken to Randall instantly, and Randall, of course, lapped up the attention, causing her to feel more on the outside than ever. Sighing, she skewered the last bit of chicken and washed her hands. Then looked around to see what was left to do.

Geena handed her a frothy pink daiquiri. "Smile,

sweetie. Life is too short to worry about the things you can't change.''

Kelly took a sip and followed her sister's instructions. She really ought to try to relax more. Oddly enough, smiling *did* make her feel better. Though she still had to put out the condiments and napkins... ''Do you think the guys want a daiquiri?''

Through the floor-to-ceiling windows in the family room she could see the three men clustered around the barbecue, which Max had positioned next to a picnic table overlooking the river. Her gaze homed in on Max, tall and athletic, fair head thrown back in laughter. Being apart hurt. It hurt so bad.

Her daughters—even Robyn—Randall and Miranda were throwing the Frisbee around on the wide lawn. Billy and Flora ran back and forth, pouncing like bandits on any missed catch.

Erin joined her at the window. ''I know Nick is happier with beer.''

''Ben, too—'' Geena said, then went quiet, a hand to her ear. ''Whose baby is that?''

The four women cocked their heads to listen and the second little one started up. Geena and Erin looked at each other and smiled.

''Well, what did we expect, putting them to nap side by side in the living room?'' Erin said.

Geena glanced at her watch. "Sonja's going to need a feed."

"Erik, too," Erin said. "That boy is always hungry."

Somewhat wistfully, Kelly watched her sisters go off to attend to their offspring. It would have been fun to be caring for a baby when her sisters were caring for theirs.

Gran put the last cut roll on the stack. "Anything else need doing?"

Kelly set mustard and ketchup on the table where plates and cutlery were laid out buffet-style. Salads, rolls, chips. The meat was ready to go on the coals…. "No, looks like we're done for now. Go on outside and enjoy the sunshine."

"I will." Gran rose from her chair with the help of her cane. "Why don't you join me. You need to get out of the kitchen."

"I'll just tidy up a bit and be right out." Kelly whisked away one of the twins' ride-on toys as Gran negotiated her way around the table. "Do you want me to carry your drink?"

"I can manage." Gran demonstrated by hanging her cane on the back of a chair and walking through the open sliding doors onto the patio under her own steam.

Max, who was just coming in, waited for her to

go through. He watched her progress to the group of lawn chairs set up for the adults, then turned to Kelly. "She gets around pretty good for a crippled woman."

"She's much better," Kelly admitted. As usual, she was full of conflicting emotions where Max was concerned: irritation rising from his constant needling, guilt because she knew he was right and frustration for their inability to restore physical and emotional closeness. She was about to tell him that in spite of Gran's recovery she still wasn't ready to come home, when her resistance crumbled and all she wanted was to connect. Touching his arm, she said, "Everybody really likes Randall."

Max's face brightened to a degree she hadn't seen in years, possibly not since the twins were born. "He's really enjoying having so much family."

"I'm surprised you didn't invite your parents," she said, both loving and hating him for his paternal devotion. "Surely Randall would have liked to meet his grandparents."

"I did." Max said shortly. "They wouldn't come."

Ouch, she winced, angry on his behalf. She'd have thought her in-laws would overlook the circumstances of Randall's birth, especially since he was their only grandson.

Arms crossed over his dark blue shirt, Max leaned against the counter, his pensive gaze fixed on the playing children.

"I know you missed not having brothers and sisters, but you can't live through Randall, Max," she said gently. "Nor can you change the course of his life."

He turned his head to look at her. "I already have."

Kelly felt a chill down her spine. She faced the sink and began running water over the dishes used in food preparation. It was true. The girls, Max, even their family and friends...*all* their lives had been changed forever by Randall's coming here. She herself had been jolted out of her comfort zone and the change wasn't for the better.

But she'd decided this morning she wouldn't spoil today by arguing, even if she had to pretend nothing was wrong.

"I need to apologize to you," she said over the clatter of dishes and running water.

"Pardon?" Max leaned toward her, an amused smile playing over his face. "Did you say 'apologize'?"

Kelly rolled her eyes at the obvious relish in his voice. "You'll never believe who I saw this morning with their heads together. Robyn and Randall. I could have sworn she hated him—sorry, disliked him intensely—but they've been spending a lot of time together lately.''

''I know,'' Max said, frowning a little. ''I'm pleased, but it *is* odd. What happened, do you think?''

''Perhaps it was their little plot. Remember how I got mad at you for buying so many flowers for me?''

His features hardened slightly. ''Yes—''

''I received *two* huge bouquets that morning,'' she went on hurriedly before he could add something she wouldn't be able to overlook.

''*Two?* But I only bought one. Who—? You mean *Robyn and Randall?*'' She nodded. His eyebrows rose as he whistled through his teeth. ''No wonder you said I was too extravagant.''

''They signed theirs from 'A Not-So-Secret Admirer.' I looked at the card and believed it was your handwriting, clumsily disguised. Randall's is remarkably similar.''

''Is that right? I hadn't noticed.'' Max seemed ridiculously pleased. ''I always thought handwriting was one of those completely individual things.''

''There appear to be family traits. Look at Erin, Geena and me—each of us has distinctive writing, yet we all make similar loops on our *g*s and *y*s.''

"Just as I always suspected—you're a set of evil triplets."

Kelly gave him a you're-so-funny smirk and nudged him aside so she could stack a clean pot in the draining tray. She slipped him a sideways smile. "I'm sorry I was so ungracious at the time. I'm not sure I even thanked you properly for the flowers."

His gaze met hers, tender and humorous. "Just tell me mine were the nicest." She nodded, and he seemed satisfied, then a second later he shook his head with a puzzled frown. "Why would Robyn and Randall do that?"

"Isn't it obvious? They wanted me to think the flowers were from you, little knowing you'd already sent me some."

"They shouldn't have been so sneaky, but you've got to admit, their hearts were in the right place."

"Yeah, I guess. Though I don't see what they thought they were going to achieve."

She waited for Max to say, "You coming home," but he didn't. The silence extended. Max glanced away. Kelly reached for the chef's knife and plunged it into the dishwater.

"Why are you washing dishes now?" he asked. "Surely that can wait. Later, I'll help. The kids will help."

"I just want to get some of the mess out of the

way. You can start barbecuing anytime. I won't be long.''

"In a minute." Max moved closer. "I want to thank *you*, Kel, for going along with this." He swept an arm wide, indicating the food, the family get-together, the whole day.

She shrugged, her arms in soapy water, her hair fallen forward, shielding her face. Pretending nothing was wrong wasn't so bad. It made things feel almost normal.

Except that she and Max hadn't touched each other in weeks. There was nothing normal about that.

"And I want to tell you my good news," he continued. Her eyebrows rose and he broke into a broad smile. "The preliminary round of judging is over. I've been nominated for the Stonington."

"Oh, Max!" Disregarding her soapy, wet hands she threw them around his neck and kissed him. "Congratulations. I knew you could do it."

"The awards dinner is coming up in two weeks." Max slid his arms around her waist. "I'd really like you to be with me on the night."

"I wouldn't miss it." Noticing damp patches on his shirt, she laughed and started to pull away. "I'm getting you all wet."

Instead of letting her go, he tightened his arms around her waist. His intense blue gaze filled her vision and she couldn't look away, even though she knew he could see the naked longing in her eyes. Then he dropped his head and a sigh quivered through her as his mouth met hers in a kiss so sweet and tender and full of love she could have cried.

When at last she dragged herself back, a shaky smile tugged at her mouth. "I didn't see that one coming."

His fingertips lightly touched the dimple in her right cheek. "We're good together, Kel."

Once more she waited for him to ask her to return home. And maybe this time she would have said yes. Instead, he kissed her again, long and deep, until her knees started to soften and she melted against him. His hand cupped her breast and her body came alive with his touch—

"Excuse me," someone said.

CHAPTER TEN

RANDALL'S VOICE YANKED Kelly back to dirty dishwater and granite benchtops.

"Tina and Tammy want me to take them out in the boat—" he continued, then broke off as he suddenly realized what they'd been doing. "Oh! Sorry." His face brick red, he stumbled backward onto the patio.

Unperturbed, Max said, "Sure, Randall. The life jackets are in the garage. Make sure the girls wear them." Randall ran off and Max turned back to Kelly. "Where were we?"

Kelly damped down the pulsing of blood in her veins. All her alarm bells were ringing. "Are you sure it's a good idea for him to take out the little ones? Does he even know how to drive a boat?"

"I've been teaching him," Max said. "Don't worry so much. Puttering around in a sixteen-foot aluminum boat with a fifty-horsepower motor is not exactly the stuff of Evel Knievel." He slid one hand around to grasp hers and attempted to dance her out of the kitchen. "Come and join the party."

"Pretty smooth moves, mister," she purred, adapting her steps to his. "Have you been taking lessons?"

He chuckled. "I've got moves you've never *imagined*."

At the table, Kelly slipped out of his arms. "You take the platter of chicken and hamburgers and I'll bring the salads." Kelly removed her apron, loaded herself up with bowls and followed Max outside.

She was a quarter of the way across the lawn when she saw Tina and Tammy scamper down the short dock and into the boat. They were not wearing life jackets. The tiny craft bobbed wildly, sending wavelets lapping at the pilings.

"I'll be a pirate princess, Tammy, and you can be a mermaid," Tina said, her excited voice carrying easily.

"Ooh, goody. I'm Ariel," Tammy crowed. Then she planted her little fists firmly on her hips. "Only, I'm not going on land 'cuz then I can't talk."

"Okay," Tina said. "Oh, I know. You'll take me to your underwater kingdom and show me your treasure."

Tammy scrambled to the side of the boat and hung

over the edge, her small bottom waggling in the air.
"I can see the castle. Tina, look!"

Dear God, Kelly thought, they hadn't even left the
dock and they were already in danger.

"Tina! Tammy!" she yelled. "Get all the way inside the boat and sit properly!"

Nick and Ben, alerted by her voice, looked up.
They took a few steps toward the dock. Max, jaw
set, strode across the lawn, his gaze on the twins. He
didn't notice a chicken shish kebab fall off the platter, to be quickly gobbled up by Billy.

Randall hurried past Kelly on his way down to the
water, fluorescent orange life jackets dangling from
his arm. "Hey, kids. You were supposed to put these
on before you got in the boat."

Either they didn't hear him or they didn't want to
obey. Tina moved to Tammy's side and leaned over
the low gunwale. The boat, which was attached by a
painter to a ring on the dock, swung away from its
mooring into midstream.

"Where's the castle?" Tina demanded of her sister.

"There," Tammy said, pointing into the murky
water. "Can't you see it?"

Tina leaned farther over. The boat tilted dangerously.

"Tina!" Kelly shrieked.

Randall dropped the life jackets and ran the last few steps to the boat. He lunged for the painter, but his sharp jerk on the rope tipped Tina off balance. With a yelp of surprise, she somersaulted into the water. And sank out of sight.

Kelly screamed.

Randall dove in after Tina.

Kelly dropped the bowls of salad on the lawn and ran toward the water. She heard Max swear, saw him shove the meat platter into Ben's hands and race for the dock. Tammy shrank back into the bottom of the boat, her little face white and terrified.

Kelly tore after Max. *Please, God, please. Don't let her drown.* The river was murky, the bottom current swift, and Tina could barely dog-paddle in the shallows. *God,* please *don't let her drown.*

Randall surfaced ten yards downstream, gasping for breath, blood pouring from his forehead. Flicking wet hair from his eyes, he glanced wildly around, then dove again.

By this time, Max had reached the end of the dock. He kicked off his shoes and was about to dive in, when Randall surfaced, a limp and dripping little girl in his arms. He swam back to the dock, keeping Tina's head above water.

"I don't think she's breathing," Randall gasped.

"Give her to me, son." Max reached down and Randall handed Tina up.

Anger surged through Kelly, replacing the intense fear of moments ago. Anger so fierce and overwhelming she nearly lost control. How could Max call him 'son' when he'd almost drowned their daughter?

Then the sight of Tina lying inert on the dock displaced those feelings and brought Kelly to her knees. "Oh, Max! Our baby."

Ben ran forward and Max moved aside to let him take over. Ben checked for a pulse, rolled Tina on her side to clear her airway and began mouth-to-mouth resuscitation. Max crouched on Tina's other side, ready to assist if necessary.

Nick pulled the boat to the dock and scooped Tammy out. "Take her up to the house," he ordered Miranda. "Beth and Robyn go, too. Call 911."

"I wanna stay with Tina," Tammy wailed, but Miranda picked her up and carried her away.

Kelly stuffed her hand in her mouth to quell her wrenching sobs. Her sisters wove their arms around her on either side and held her tightly, uttering soothing words of hope and support.

Maybe only thirty seconds had passed since Ben had begun resuscitation, but to Kelly it seemed an eternity. Then she heard Tina cough and splutter back to life. Kelly sobbed with relief and ran to her daughter. Tina curled up in her mother's arms and immediately began to cry. A protective arm around Kelly, Max touched Tina's hair, her arm, her foot, as if convincing himself she was alive.

Randall hauled himself from the water, dripping wet. His head throbbed and his lungs ached, but those pains were minor compared with the hurt in his heart from the accusing glare Kelly had flung at him. She probably didn't even realize she'd done it, but he knew she blamed him for Tina's accident.

Tina was safe. That was all that mattered, he told himself, trying to shake off a debilitating sense of rejection. He wasn't looking for a mother. He *had* a mother. A mother who loved him just as much as Kelly loved her daughters. He had a father, too, although Max was something special.

Kelly started back to the house with Tina. Max came up to Randall and put his arm around him, heedless of Randall's soaking clothes. "That was a brave thing you did, jumping into the river after Tina," he said. "She's going to be fine thanks to you."

Randall began to feel a little better. "I didn't think about it. I just did it."

Max pushed aside lank, wet hair to examine his forehead. "The cut has nearly stopped bleeding."

Ben came over and had a look. "Just a bad graze. You won't need stitches." He paused at the sound of a siren.

"I'll take care of that," Nick said, and headed off.

"Get out of those wet clothes, Randall, and I'll find something in my bag of tricks to patch you up," Ben added, clapping a hand on his shoulder. "First I want to have another look at Tina."

Randall trudged up the slope to the house and went in through the laundry room door so he wouldn't drip on the carpet. He stripped off his wet clothes and pulled a towel from the linen closet to wrap around his waist. Holding a clean rag to his forehead to stanch the blood, he peered down the hall. No one in sight.

From the bathroom came voices and the splash of bathwater. Kelly and Tina; one gently scolding, one explaining in earnest tones why the unexpected dip in the river wasn't her fault.

"Tammy said there was a castle down there. Ariel's castle."

"She probably saw some old pilings," Kelly told Tina. "Don't you ever do that again."

On his way past the bathroom Kelly poked her head around the door. "Randall, wait." She wrapped Tina in a big towel and said, "Go get dressed." The little girl ran down the hall.

Randall, left facing Kelly, mumbled, "I'm sorry about the accident. Is Tina okay?"

"She's fine." Kelly's gaze went to his bleeding forehead. "Let me see that."

He lifted the cloth away from his forehead and she stood on tiptoes to peer at the cut. "You must have scraped your head on the submerged pilings. Hang on."

"Ben'll look at it..." Randall began, but Kelly had already gone back into the bathroom. She returned with a first-aid kit and led him into the living room. "Sit."

Randall sat on a stool, feeling horribly self-conscious about being clad only in a towel. Kelly didn't seem to notice, or even see him.

"A mother knows almost as much about patching up kids as a doctor," she said, dabbing antiseptic on the wound.

Randall had nothing to say to that. She wasn't *his* mother. He didn't understand why she was doing this. Or why the fingers that applied the bandage to his forehead were gentle and the eyes that met his, as she drew back, kind.

"Thank you for saving my little girl," she said, her voice husky.

Randall nodded, wanting to believe she meant it.

"I shouldn't have let them go near the dock without their life jackets on. It was my fault—"

"No, it wasn't. Max has drilled water safety into them since they could understand speech. They knew better." Her gaze downcast, she crumpled the paper wrapping the bandage had come in. "I reacted badly on the dock. I may have looked at you in a way that was hurtful to you. I'm sorry."

He nodded again, his heart listening. "It's okay."

Kelly gathered up the first-aid kit and rose. Randall got up, too, clutching his towel. At the door, she turned. "By the way, thanks for the flowers you and Robyn sent."

Frozen in his tracks, he waited for her to tell him off. But she simply gave him a brief ironic smile and walked out, leaving him scratching the unwounded side of his head. "Not-So-Secret" was right. How the heck had she figured it out?

"HI, DR. JOHNSON," Kelly said to her OB-GYN, hopping onto the examining table. She was here to have another IUD inserted. Max's awards night was next week and she wanted to be prepared. Just in case.

"Good to see you, Kelly," Dr. Johnson greeted her warmly. The kindly white-haired doctor had not only delivered Kelly's four daughters but also Kelly and her sisters. Even though he and his young partner had moved offices from Everett into the new medical center in downtown Seattle, she didn't mind the longer trip necessary to see him.

After the preliminary courtesies were out of the way, Dr. Johnson donned a pair of latex gloves and asked, "How long since your last period?"

"To tell you the truth, I'm not sure." As she lay down on the examining table, she frowned, thinking back. Good grief. Unless she counted the spotting in early June, her last real period had occurred before she and Max went to the Salish Lodge. "Um, the beginning of May, I think." Since it was now the last week in July she couldn't blame Dr. Johnson's bushy white eyebrows for rising above his gold-rimmed glasses. Kelly hastened to explain, "I've been going through a pretty stressful time this summer and missed a period. Maybe two. Does it matter?"

"I can't insert an IUD while you're menstruating. The wall of the uterus is soft and could be damaged. I'll do an internal examination, and if everything looks okay I'll go ahead. Just place your feet in the stirrups."

Kelly turned her gaze to the ceiling and breathed deeply and slowly while Dr. Johnson inserted the speculum and conducted an internal. After only a minute, he pushed his chair away from the end of the table and rose to continue his examination by palpating her abdomen.

"Well, Kelly, it looks as though you won't be able to have that IUD after all."

"Why not?" Kelly said, disappointed. "Am I too close to my period?"

"No." Dr. Johnson's pale blue eyes regarded her kindly. "But an IUD at this stage would be like shutting the proverbial barn door after the horse has bolted." He withdrew his hands and smiled genially. "You're pregnant."

The air stopped in her lungs. For a moment Kelly thought she was going to black out. Forcing in a deep breath, she propped herself up on her elbow. "My periods have always been irregular, and I've missed before due to stress. Could you be mistaken?"

He shook his head. "Not a chance."

"But...but...I *can't* be pregnant," she wailed as the full impact hit her. "I have too much to do with my life."

She fell back on the table and put her hands over her face. *Pregnant!* Periods aside, she'd never experienced a day of morning sickness in her life, and she'd been too busy to notice other, more subtle changes in her body. This was a disaster.

Dr. Johnson peeled off his latex gloves and disposed of them in the wastebasket. "Max will be pleased," he went on cheerfully. "I recall him telling me when the twins were born that he wanted more children."

Kelly moaned. Max wouldn't merely be pleased; he'd be ecstatic. Unless, perhaps, the baby was born a girl. In spite of his protestations, she was sure he was hoping for a boy next time. If there was a next time. "I knew I should have had my tubes tied after the twins."

Dr. Johnson frowned thoughtfully. "I take it *you* don't welcome the news. There's no medical reason you can't deliver a child. But of course, the decision to go ahead with the pregnancy is one only you and Max can make."

Unless she didn't tell Max. Prickles of cold sweat popped out across her hairline. "When is the baby due?"

"Let's see. Say the first day of your last period was the first week of May, then—" he consulted a chart matching conception dates with due dates "—you should be due on February 5 next year. Or thereabouts."

February. A time when she should be getting ready for the spring surge in real estate listings and poring over seed catalogs, not changing diapers and breast-feeding. She sighed. Somehow she would just have to manage to do it all. *Damn.* Why hadn't she and Max been more careful at the lodge?

"You're a natural mother, Kelly." Dr. Johnson placed a comforting hand on her shoulder and squeezed. "Once you're over the initial surprise I'm sure you'll see this pregnancy in a more positive light."

Kelly managed a grim smile. She wished *she* could be so sure of that. At the moment all she could feel was outrage at the loss of her independence.

"You can get dressed now." Dr. Johnson moved toward the door. "Before you leave, make an appointment with my receptionist for three weeks from now. We'll do an ultrasound to confirm the due date and make sure everything's okay."

He was about to close the door when she called, "Oh, Doctor. If you happen to see Max, don't tell him about the baby. I'd like to do that."

"Of course."

"I FEEL LIKE CINDERELLA before the big ball." Kelly twirled in front of the full-length mirror on the back of the closet door. She wore only a slip, but already she was imagining herself the object of Max's adoring gaze. Tonight she absolutely refused to spoil her evening by thinking about her pregnancy.

Erin and Geena were with her in her old room at

Gran's house, helping her get ready for Max's award night.

"Only, instead of mean, ugly stepsisters you have beautiful, kind, generous sisters," said Erin, tongue firmly in cheek. She picked up a brush. "Come here and I'll do your hair."

"Witty, charming, adorable sisters," Geena agreed. She pushed Kelly onto the stool in front of the vanity. "I'll do your makeup."

"Bossy, fussy, annoying sisters," Kelly grumbled, succumbing to their wishes. She met their gazes in the mirror and gave a rueful grin. "But thanks. If it wasn't for you two I'd go looking like the poor housemaid."

"Prince Charming would still recognize your princess-like qualities." Erin ran the brush through Kelly's glossy chestnut hair. "How do you want it styled?"

"I don't know. Something simple." In the mirror she saw Geena and Erin exchange glances and realized she was in for a special hairstyle to match her dress.

"What time is Max picking you up?" Erin began sweeping Kelly's hair off her forehead in a series of tiny bunches, which twisted together in an intricate pattern.

"He's not." Kelly tilted her chin while Geena applied foundation with swift light strokes of her fingertips. "He has to go in early to meet with a client before the awards so I'm taking my car. But it's okay. This way I'm my own boss."

"From the way you two were smooching in the kitchen at the barbecue I thought you'd sorted yourselves out," Geena said.

Kelly rolled her eyes. "Did *everyone* see us kissing?"

"I don't know about everyone. I was bringing Sonja out and happened to catch a glimpse." Geena smiled. "Before I beat a hasty retreat."

"We *were* smooching," Kelly admitted. "And it felt pretty darn good, too."

"Has Max apologized?" Erin asked.

"Well, no, not as such…"

Erin slid a clip into the knot of hair atop Kelly's head. "Has he agreed to counseling?"

"Not exactly…"

Erin stopped what she was doing and fixed Kelly with a stern gaze, silently demanding to know why she'd let down her standards.

"Oh, for God's sake!" Kelly cried. "I miss him!"

"Of course you do, sweetie," Geena said, glaring at Erin. "Kiss and make up. *Then* sort out your problems."

Erin stared at Geena. "*You've* sure changed your

tune.'' She shook her head, divesting herself of responsibility. ''You lose power when you give in so easily,'' she said to Kelly around a mouthful of bobby pins. ''Power you'll never get back.''

''Do you and Nick engage in power struggles in your relationship?'' Geena demanded.

''Well, no...'' Erin looked sheepish. ''I guess I was thinking of John,'' she said, referring to her former fiancé.

''Didn't think you were talking about Nick.'' Geena chose a dark brown eyeliner from her cosmetic case and proceeded to smudge it below Kelly's eyes. ''Follow your heart, Kel. If you want to make up with Max it's your business.''

''Of course it is,'' Erin conceded. ''I'm sure he'd be thrilled.''

''I hope so.'' Kelly's reflected expression turned a little anxious. He would be thrilled if she told him about the baby— *Stop!* She wasn't going to think about that.

''You don't believe he'll welcome you back?'' Erin gave a scoffing snort of laughter. ''He'll jump for joy.''

''I don't know about that. It's been weeks since he asked me to come home. Maybe he doesn't want me back anymore.''

Erin and Geena were silent a moment, digesting this. Then they both began to talk at once.

"It means nothing."

"He loves you."

"He needs you."

Kelly looked from one sister to the other. They sounded confident, but then, they didn't know about the added complication of the baby. She wanted desperately to confide in them, but she knew if she did, she'd start crying and ruin not only Geena's makeup job but also her mood for the rest of the evening.

"You're probably right." She faced the mirror and forced herself to smile. Immediately she felt braver.

Thirty minutes later, Erin and Geena pronounced her "done." Geena went to the closet and tore away the dry-cleaning plastic from the Schiaparelli gown. She held it out for Kelly to step into.

"Turn around and breathe in, sweetie, while I do up the zipper."

Kelly stood before the mirror and viewed the unfamiliar yet undeniably gorgeous woman in the antique dress. No doubt about it. Max was going to be mightily impressed.

"Absolutely stunning," Erin pronounced, then searched the closet for the slingbacks.

Kelly grimaced at the designer shoes. "They're so

high. And pointy. My toes will be killing me by the end of the evening.''

''All the more reason for Max to sweep you off your feet and into the bedroom,'' Geena replied. ''Don't be a baby. Put them on.''

Kelly slipped her feet into the sparkly fuchsia slingbacks and clicked her high heels together. ''There's no place like home.''

CHAPTER ELEVEN

MAX PACED THE GLITTERING lobby of the Alexis Hotel and for the hundredth time that evening glanced at the row of clocks over the reception desk. If they were in Honolulu the awards dinner wouldn't start for hours. But this was Seattle and Kelly was forty minutes late!

Couples in evening dress had been steadily filing from the bar into the dining room for the past half hour, their cocktail-lubricated laughter a jarring counterpoint to Max's edgy nerves.

She wasn't coming. She'd had second thoughts and decided she had no wish to celebrate the success of a man who put his long-lost son before his wife.

No, he thought, turning at the elaborate floral arrangement in the center of the lobby and heading back toward the entrance. Kelly wouldn't back out, not when she knew how much this night meant to him. Besides, she *had* to be here. He had it fixed in his head that if she came, he would win the Stonington. Conversely, since he felt so sure of winning, it stood to reason she must be coming.

Something must have happened to her on the way to the hotel. He tried her cell phone again. She still wasn't answering. Was she hurt? Lost?

"Coming in, Max?" Ross Webster, the chairman of the Architects' Association, paused on his way to the dining room.

"Soon. Just waiting for my wife." He smiled casually, as if she were in the ladies' room and would be out in a second.

"Don't wait too long. The ceremony will be starting momentarily. Can't have our star nominee miss the show." Ross clapped him on the back and moved off to join the crowd filtering through the doorway.

"She'll be here," Max muttered as if it were a mantra, and resumed pacing. "She'll be—"

"Max!"

He spun toward the revolving door. A tall, beautiful woman with upswept dark hair, in a dress that was at once sexy and elegant, entered the lobby. A beautiful woman who looked strangely like his wife. *"Kelly?"*

She tottered forward and collapsed in his arms. "Thank God, I made it. I'm just about dead."

"What happened? Where are you hurt?" He searched her for cuts or bruises.

"My feet." Leaning on him, she pulled a foot out of one elegant shoe and rubbed the reddened toes. "I was in such a hurry to get here I didn't take time to fill up on gas. I ran out fourteen blocks away on Bell Street and Third Avenue. *Fourteen blocks in four-inch heels.*"

"That sounds like a country-and-western song," Max said, amused.

She punched him in the cummerbund. "Don't you dare laugh. Could I get a cab?" she went on, speaking rhetorically. "Not for love nor money. Although one inebriated clown asked if I gave love *for* money—or words to that effect—but I passed." Finally stopping for breath, she looked him up and down. "Maxwell Walker, you are one fine specimen of a man in that tuxedo. I didn't realize I was married to such a good-looking guy."

"And you resemble a 1920s movie star. I hardly knew you when you walked in." Even now, he felt he was escorting a strange-and-exotic creature, someone he'd met for the first time tonight. The thought was intriguing. "Did Geena take you shopping?"

"She loaned me this dress. And I will never wear it again, not if it means putting on these torture chambers called high-fashion shoes. I don't know how Geena and Erin do it."

"They don't have your good sense. But I have to

admit, you look wonderful tonight, Kel. You do me proud." He tucked her arm through his. "We'd better go in. Can you walk?"

"Through coals if necessary." Tilting her face, she smiled her engaging smile up at him. "I want to see you win."

"Cross your fingers, then."

"Hey, these shoes are so tight my *toes* are crossed."

In the dining room they were seated at a round table with four other couples, two of whom Max knew. Although a bottle of pinot noir and one of chardonnay were supplied, Max bought a magnum of Dom Pérignon and ordered it to be served to everyone at their table.

"Max!" Kelly chastised him under her breath. "A *magnum?*" To the waiter she said, "Just half a glass, please."

Max took her hand and touched her knuckles to his lips. "Kelly, my love, it's not every day I get nominated for the top award on the West Coast. I'm going to enjoy it to the 'max.' Pardon the pun."

A corner of Kelly's mouth lifted in an indulgent smile. "You're already drunk—on excitement."

Appetizers arrived, followed by a salad, then the main course. Wine flowed, conversation bubbled, laughter came easily. Despite Max's fears that waiting for the awards portion of the evening would make dinner seem interminable, the meal passed quickly enough. Champagne and fresh salmon helped, as did the knowledge that Kelly was at his side, where she belonged. He ate with his left hand and kept his right firmly wrapped around Kelly's.

Once dessert was served, the emcee tapped a microphone and all heads turned to the stage.

"This is it!" Kelly whispered excitedly, and squeezed Max's hand beneath the table.

First there were the speeches. Then the honorary awards. And more speeches. Finally, the awards themselves. Kelly consulted her program every two minutes, even though Max had told her many times his category was last.

"Patience," he admonished Kelly under his breath when she fidgeted throughout the early-award categories.

"I never was good at being patient," she muttered. "I wish I'd gotten a chance to look at the entries of the other finalists."

She was referring to the display set up in another room with photographs of the nominees' finished designs. "We can look later," he assured her.

"And last, but definitely not least," the emcee announced, "the category that has the architectural community from San Diego to Bellingham abuzz—

Best Luxury Domicile. Nominees are Thomas Shane, Sigrid Newstadt, Max Walker and Wallace Trenton.''

Max's colleague leaned across the table. ''You're a shoe-in.''

Max shrugged and smiled, acknowledging the compliment. ''It's enough just to be nominated.''

Of course he didn't really mean that. Winning was everything. Not that he was worried about the outcome of tonight's awards. Champagne had given him a warm, euphoric feeling, and with it the certain knowledge that imminent victory was his. He had his acceptance speech in his pocket and he had it memorized cold.

A curvaceous blonde in an evening gown glided across the stage and handed the emcee an envelope. Max shifted to the edge of his seat, ready to get to his feet and walk the walk of fame.

''And the winner is…'' The emcee tore open the envelope, scanned the contents, then leaned forward to the microphone. ''Wallace Trenton, of Trenton Designs!''

Max started to rise to thunderous applause. He froze in midair as belatedly, the announcement sank in. He hadn't won. Stunned, he ignominiously dropped back to his seat. How had this happened?

He glanced around for Kelly. She *was* here.

And she was looking at him with the most sympathetic expression imaginable in her dark brown eyes.

"Oh, Max," she said, laying a hand on his arm. "I'm so sorry."

"Doesn't matter." That gruff voice wasn't his; it was that of a loser. *Sorry,* she'd said. *Sorry.* He didn't want sympathy! He wanted adoration. Not from his peers; he didn't care about them. He *did* care about Kelly and what she thought of him.

Most of all, his acceptance speech read, *I'd like to thank my light, my life, my beautiful wife, Kelly, who has supported me and believed in me all these years. She is everything to me, and without her, I wouldn't be standing here today.*

If he'd had a chance to speak those words in his moment of triumph she'd have known just how much she meant to him. It would have, in a small way, paid her back for all she'd put up with for him to reach this point in his career, especially for placing her own dreams on hold. Heat pricked the backs of his eyes. He'd had his shot at the prize. And failed.

The same colleague who'd earlier told him he was a shoe-in threw him a commiserating grimace. "You were robbed."

Max shrugged again, his shoulders stiff with humiliation. "Wallace Trenton came up with a fantastic design. He deserves to win."

All the nominees did, when it came down to it. But surely no one had *wanted* to win more than Max. Or felt his loss more keenly. Gripped by envy and regret, he watched Wallace Trenton accept the slender chrome statuette and warmly applauded the winner along with everyone else.

He slumped back in his chair. After all the buildup, the hype, the months of hard work and weeks of anticipation, it was over. Around him, diners drained their glasses, waiters cleared away dirty dishes, people rose and began to drift out of the room. Max sat where he was, feeling as flat as the dregs of morning-after champagne.

"Max, are you all right?" Kelly's polished fingernails gleamed against the black fabric sleeve of his tux.

He gave her a brittle smile. "I'm fine."

"You don't look fine. You look pale."

Even worse than failing would be to act like a sore loser. From some unknown storehouse of inner strength Max summoned a nonchalant shrug.

Kelly didn't appear convinced. "I guess you would have liked Randall to know you won the award," she said, speaking carefully. "It would have been quite an achievement. Something to make him proud of you.''

Max stared at her. For someone who knew him so well, she sure had got it wrong. "Kelly, I—"

"You don't have to worry." She slid her hand down his arm to grip his hand, as if he were in danger of flying away. "The boy worships you. You couldn't get any more perfect in his eyes."

His throat thickened with love for her. In spite of her resentment of Randall, she cared enough to acknowledge the bond between his son and him. Max handed her the index card on which he'd written his acceptance speech.

She took it, eyeing him curiously, and as she read, a tear dropped onto the card, smearing the ink. When she glanced up, all the love he'd been longing for was in her eyes. She threw her arms around his neck. "Oh, Max, you idiot. You don't need to prove anything to me."

Max buried his face in her neck. Everything that was right and good in his life was in his arms. Why did he hurt her by wanting more? Why this deep-seated need for a son?

She must have interpreted his silence as an expression of disbelief. Drawing back, she pushed her hands through his thick hair and held his head to look directly into his eyes. "I was proud of you when you were nominated for this award. I thought it was only what you deserved. I still think that. But there've been other times I've been even prouder.''

He raised his eyebrows at that. Thus far, the Stonington Award nomination had been the biggest thing in his career. ''Like when?''

''Like when you waived the fees for designing the new maternity ward on the Hainesville Hospital. Despite the Ladies' Auxiliary and Greta Vogler's fund-raising efforts and a grant from the town council, construction would have been delayed another year without your generosity.''

''No one's supposed to hear about that,'' he reminded her. ''Or every organization in the county will be after me to waive fees.''

''I haven't said anything,'' she reassured him with a pat on the chest. ''I never even told Geena and Erin.'' At his look of surprise, she added, ''You asked me not to. Although I've always wondered why the maternity wing?''

He shrugged. ''Your sisters were starting to have children. It was a gesture.''

''That no one is allowed to appreciate you for.'' Shaking her head, she laughed softly. ''Typical Max. I was also proud of you the time I took off on short notice to the Seychelles with Geena. You weren't happy about it, but you looked after the kids without a murmur so I could have a holiday.''

He *hadn't* been happy about that and he still resented Geena a little for giving his wife a vacation he couldn't afford. There was nothing good he could say here, so he kept quiet.

Kelly didn't seem to notice. ''And then there was the time you gave up courtside tickets to the Super Sonics championship game because Beth had pneumonia and it was all I could do to take care of two-week-old twins who ate and slept at different times.''

''My six-year-old was desperately sick and you were up around the clock with newborns. What kind of guy would I have been if I'd left you alone and gone to a basketball game?''

''Not the man I married. And that's my point exactly. You put your family first even when it means personal sacrifice. Then there was the time—''

''You'd better stop before I get a swelled head.'' He rose and pulled her to her feet, linking an arm around her waist. The truth was, his heart had swelled, instead, with love and gratitude. Caught up in the daily routine, a man sometimes wondered if his efforts were appreciated. To know they were was nice.

''Okay,'' she said, hugging him. ''But if I was handing out awards I'd give you the grand prize.''

Max touched her lips lightly with his, resisting the urge to deepen the kiss. Here, among the cleaning staff and handful of lingering diners, was no place to prolong this warmth and intimacy. "Let's leave," he said huskily, "and go where we can be alone."

Kelly gathered up her purse and, with a grimace, pushed her feet back into her shoes. "I just hope we don't have to walk too far."

He took her arm, supporting her painful walk. "How does a corner suite with a Jacuzzi and a harbor view sound?"

"Like heaven." She stared at him. "Don't tell me you have one of those tucked away somewhere?"

His smile was half smug, half sheepish. "I was pretty certain I was going to win and was prepared to celebrate."

She paused in the lobby next to the elevators. "Were you also certain I would stay overnight with you?"

He sobered. "I was not." Cupping her cheek in his palm, he bent to kiss her, savoring the sweet warmth of her lips. "Will you, Kelly? I've been so lonely for you."

Kelly looked into blue eyes darkened with desire and her heart's rhythm quickened. She'd told herself she wouldn't give in, but tonight saying yes didn't feel like giving in; it felt like giving *to* him. And

receiving. The sentiments expressed in his acceptance speech had been a gift, unexpected and, considering her behavior these past weeks, somewhat
undeserved. But then, Max always had been generous with love.

"I will."

With a whoop, Max swept her up in his arms and
whirled around to punch the elevator button. One
high-heel shoe flew off.

"Max! Put me down." She shrieked with laughter.
"You can't carry me all the way to our hotel room."

"That's for sure." The elevator doors opened and
he deposited her inside. He grabbed her shoe and
stepped in himself just before the doors slid closed.

They were alone. And Max had a look in his eyes
she hadn't seen since they were newlyweds. Too late,
Kelly started having second thoughts about the wis-
dom of this impulsive overnighter. "What about the
kids?"

"I told them we'd probably stay in town and arranged for Nancy to come over. Don't even think
about the kids tonight."

"What'll I do for a change of clothes?" she protested. "I didn't bring so much as a toothbrush."

"Beautiful women in designer dresses don't worry
about where their next toothbrush is coming from."

He backed her against the wall, his tall, athletic

frame looming over her with an air of authority that was dangerously attractive. This whole scenario was so far outside their usual routine, it was exciting and unfamiliar and...seductive.

"Who *are* you?" she murmured.

He dropped kisses down her throat as his hands settled on the curve of her hips. "I'm the man who's going to make love to you."

A delicious shiver ran down her spine and she tilted her face, asking to be kissed. He took her mouth with a ruthlessness unlike the Max she knew. When her stomach dropped she wasn't sure whether it was from the swift rise of the elevator or the suggestive foreplay of his tongue. His large hands moved restlessly over the delicate silk of her gown. She could easily pretend they were two strangers, powerfully attracted and fated to be together, ready to abandon all responsibility to make passionate love in a luxury hotel suite.

Or an elevator. Kelly was a heartbeat away from pushing the stop button, when the elevator made a little *ding* and came to a halt of its own accord.

Max led her a short way down the corridor and paused to open the hotel suite with a card key. Then he scooped her up and carried her over the threshold.

The room was unlit but for a small table lamp next to a floral arrangement that gave off enough scent to make her giddy. The undraped windows displayed an expanse of glittering lights, bisected by a dark finger of Puget Sound. A fairy-tale setting for what was turning out to be a fairy-tale evening.

"Oh, Max," she said as he set her back on her feet. "This is fantastic." Extravagant, too, so soon after their weekend in Snoqualmie, but she didn't care and she certainly wasn't going to break the spell by mentioning one word about the expense.

"Champagne?" He indicated an ice bucket and two flutes next to the flowers.

"I've had enough to drink." She'd nursed half a glass through dinner, not wanting to risk harm to the baby. Sliding a hand inside his jacket, she murmured, "I want *you*."

"Babe, I'm yours." He shed his tux jacket and loosened his tie with a look in his eyes that dried her throat.

She reached behind her neck to undo the row of tiny buttons, but he shook his head.

"Turn around," he ordered. And she did.

Kelly trembled as the buttons fell away beneath his fingers, and instead of silk, Max's warm breath caressed her back. The dress fell to her waist and he turned her back to him, her arms pinned by the sleeves. His gaze dropped to her breasts, curving above rose-colored lace, and she heard his indrawn breath. Max was handsome and breathtakingly sexual. She was as nervous and excited as if this were her first time. Unlike her first time, she knew how good making love with the man she adored could be, and thrilled to the prospect.

His hands, familiar yet new, traced over her breasts until her nipples ached with the need to be squeezed. She wanted to touch him, too, but the dress had her hands trapped, leaving Max free to taste and touch and tease. She could do nothing but shiver and throb and wait for him to release her.

Max tugged her bra down, exposing one nipple, hard and erect. Kelly's eyes shut as he drew it into his mouth and sucked, released and sucked again, setting up a throbbing between her legs that threatened to buckle her knees.

"Max." She strained against the dress, just aware enough not to struggle too hard and damage the fabric.

He took pity on her, stepping back to let the dress slide down her slender hips, past matching rose-colored lace panties cut high in the leg and dipping low in front. Panties so sexy Kelly had become half aroused just putting them on. Anyone would think she'd been hoping the night would unfold in this way.

Smiling a secret smile, she captured the dress before it pooled on the floor and carefully laid it over the back of a chair. In the dresser mirror she caught a glimpse of her and Max and was mesmerized by the erotic image they made—she in her scanty lingerie, he still in dress shirt and dark pants. As she watched, he reached around from behind to cup her breasts and pressed his steel-hard erection against the softness of her buttocks.

Her knees weakened and she leaned forward, supporting her weight on the dresser. Behind her in the mirror, Max, blue eyes burning, ripped off the dangling bow tie and tore open his shirt studs. His tanned chest glowed in the lamplight, shadows forming in the hollows of his muscles. He undid her bra strap and freed her breasts, only to immediately capture them in his hands. One arm banded her chest while his other hand slipped down, beneath the front of her panties. Simultaneously seeing and feeling what he was doing turned her on and made her pleasurably confused.

But the mirror also made him seem too distant so she turned, sliding shaky hands up his chest to smooth his shirt off his shoulders. For weeks she'd longed to touch him. Now she savored the taste of him, kissing and licking until his rigid muscles quivered with the effort to maintain control. An almost painful groan erupted from his chest, and he dragged her head up to capture her mouth in a kiss so deep and long she almost forgot her own name.

Wanting more of him, she tugged his pants down. *More?* She'd certainly gotten what she asked for. This man was a colossus, powerful and sexual, who clearly wanted her in the worst way.

Suddenly, she was consumed with need. Every minute of the past three months of celibacy focused her desire on one thing—having him inside her. Taking him in both hands, she brushed her naked breasts back and forth across his chest. "I want to make love *now*."

Max groaned at the erotic sensations bewitching him. With the dropping of his trousers, the sweetly sexy woman in his arms had morphed into a sensual wildcat. Was this *Kelly?* She'd never been shy in bed, but this woman was shameless—stroking and teasing him into the biggest, hardest erection of his life. All thoughts and feelings coalesced into a single driving desire.

He tumbled her onto the bed, slid the last scrap of lace over her hips and explored with his fingers. She was slick and hot, swollen and ripe.

"Hurry, Max," she panted, parting her legs for him.

"Hang on," he gasped. "Condom."

"Never mind. Please, Max."

No condom? Okay by him. With one long, deep stroke he entered her.

He began to move inside her, establishing a rhythm, then changing it. Everything about this night had turned out unpredictably, most of all—the sex. Had he ever known Kelly to moan with such passion when he touched her just there? Had she ever taken him into her mouth with such eagerness? They experimented with every position they knew and invented more. But the tension couldn't last forever. It built and built until, he erupted in a rush of pleasure, a shattering, blinding cascade so pure and intense he lost awareness of self. Descending, he floated in a sea of primordial bliss.

When he opened his eyes, she was Kelly again and he was Max. Even better than the hot sex was their emotional closeness. They'd been estranged for too long and now they were intimate again.

"Like the first time, only better," she murmured, eyelids fluttering shut.

"Yes, better," he agreed hoarsely.

Now, there was an understatement.

KELLY AWOKE SLOWLY, filled with a warm fuzzy feeling, the cause of which she couldn't immediately place. Her eyes opened a crack, but the room was so dark she couldn't see anything. She knew she wasn't at home and she wasn't at Gran's. Then she heard the soft sound of Max breathing and, stretching a foot, encountered his leg. Ah, here was the source of the warm fuzzies. Her very own Love Machine.

The previous night came flooding back to her in sequence: the sharp sense of loss on Max's behalf, the reminders to herself and him of all the reasons she loved him and, as if that wasn't enough, the most earth-shattering lovemaking.

Had he wondered why she hadn't insisted on a condom?

Deliciously achy, fully contented, Kelly pushed the thought from her mind and luxuriously stretched her limbs. Eyes still shut, Max reached for her and she slid over and into his arms.

"Morning," she murmured, kissing his jaw.

He rumbled something in her ear and shifted so they were facing each other.

"Somebody's up early," she teased, feeling him hard against her belly.

Max opened his eyes. "He's been up most of the night, but you were snoring so loudly I didn't have the heart to wake you."

She'd been sucking on his earlobe; now she nipped with her teeth. "I do not snore."

"Do, too," he said lazily.

"Do not."

"Do, too."

"You trying to pick a fight so we can make up?" She'd missed the bantering almost as much as the lovemaking.

"No, I like you angry. You're feisty when you're angry."

"Feisty? You make me sound like a militant granny."

He laughed. "I mean, *sexy* feisty. Spunky. Like last night." His erection pressed harder.

"Mmm, I'm feeling too laid-back to be feisty this morning. But give me a back scratch and I could do languorous. I'll even purr like a cat."

"Purr away, kitty cat." Without changing position, he ran his short nails up and down her back, all over, not too hard and not too soft, just the way she liked it.

"No one scratches backs like you," she murmured, pressing kisses into his neck while she slipped a hand between them to begin a manual caress of her own.

Slow and easy, they made love. Their gazes locked; she watched pleasure suffuse his smile and his eyelids droop, heard his breath shorten and inhaled his deeply male scent.

If last night's sex had been earth-shattering, this morning's was soul-connecting. Afterward she touched her lips to the moisture rimming Max's eyes, in awe of the way he could make her feel after all these years together. Golden silence enveloped them, eliminating the need for words. She lay lost in his gaze, as he was lost in hers, sharing the same small smile that expressed so much.

Then, to Kelly's surprise, Max's smile faded. "Kelly, I...I'm sorry."

"Max, honey," she said wonderingly. "Whatever for?"

He'd never looked so open, so raw and vulnerable. "For Lanni. For hurting you. I knew that summer that you still loved me, would marry me when we had a chance. Away from you I got all mixed up. I was angry at you, afraid of losing my freedom. I loved you and at the same time I resented you for tying up my heart so completely."

Wincing at his brutal honesty, she asked, "Why did you come back to me?"

"I knew I'd never love anyone the way I loved you."

"Oh, Max." She kissed him gently on the lips.

"After my fling with Lanni I realized how much I appreciated you. How much I wanted and needed you." He paused. "I'm also sorry I never told you about Randall. That was unforgivable."

Finally, *finally,* he'd given her the apology she

needed to restore her dignity within their marriage. Her heart swelled to bursting. "Even so, I forgive you."

Eyes downcast, he trailed a fingertip along her collarbone. "Can you like Randall, do you think?"

"Oh, Max, I feel ashamed of the way I've treated him at times. He's really a sweet kid." She paused. "I just wish *I* had given you the son you always wanted."

Max rolled on his back. "It's not so important—"

"Max..."

He faced her again, his mouth strained with the difficulty of confessing. "It's not that I don't love the girls with all my heart—"

"I know. I *know*." Hand splayed against his chest, she could feel his heart beat beneath her palm. "It's okay to admit it. You want a son. And you have one. You have Randall. I won't try to keep you away from him again."

"I want *us* to have a son." He smiled. "Maybe this time."

Kelly froze, her heart in her mouth. "Wha-what do you mean?"

He tucked a strand of her hair behind her ear. "You didn't insist on a condom. I took it you'd decided you want another baby."

"No! I haven't decided any such thing!"

"Then why did you agree to unprotected sex? This time I double-checked that I had condoms. There was no excuse."

Kelly sat up in bed, clutching the sheet to her with one hand, while the other hand raked wildly through her hair. "I...I got carried away. Stopping would have spoiled the moment."

Max's face darkened as he rolled to the side of the bed and sat up, facing away from her. "Don't screw me around, Kelly. You've got to make up your mind, one way or another."

The way he said it made her think he was talking about more than just a baby; he was talking about their marriage.

She put her arms around his shoulders and laid her head on the back of his neck. "Max, I love you." She felt the deep breath that shuddered through him and clung tighter.

At last he turned and took her in his arms. "I love you, too, Kel."

They held each other, and Kelly gratefully absorbed the warmth and comfort of his arms. Then Max drew back, his eyes searching hers. "Our marriage is being tested more than I ever thought possible. We're on a cliff edge, one minute soaring, the next plummeting. We can either end it or enlarge it."

Fear entered her heart. *End it?* "I don't understand."

With gentle fingers, he smoothed the hair off her face. "To survive, we need to expand, make our relationship bigger, make our love bigger, so that it's a place of nurture and refuge. What do you say we have a fresh start? Renew our vows."

"You mean, get married again?" Tears welled in Kelly's eyes.

He nodded. "As a symbol of our willingness to keep our marriage, not just intact, but strong."

He was so noble, so strong and generous. While she kept secrets, he opened his heart. There was no question she wanted their marriage to strengthen and grow. Yet however guilty she felt about not telling him she was pregnant, doing so would commit her to having the baby. Part of her wanted another child, but she was still torn by her desire for a career. And she was afraid of Max's disappointment if they had another girl. He had to get over his need for a son of his own. Although she couldn't *make* that happen, she could love and nurture him. Provide that place of refuge.

Summoning a smile, she said, "Yes, Max. I'll marry you again—gladly."

CHAPTER TWELVE

MAX FOLLOWED THE WOMAN he loved into the house. They'd stopped at Ruth's on their way home to pick up Kelly's things and now he carried his wife's bulging suitcases in from the car. No burden ever felt so light; no task was ever performed with such joy. Kelly was home to stay.

He was frustrated she was still stalling on having another baby, but the important thing was her willingness to give their marriage another chance.

Robyn, Beth, Tina and Tammy greeted them at the door with smiles and hugs. Although they'd seen Kelly every day during her time at Ruth's, they seemed to sense that this homecoming was different. The faint atmosphere of gloom that had descended over the house while she'd been away lifted, and celebration was in the air.

Max noticed that Randall, possibly still unsure of his welcome, hung back, allowing Kelly time with her daughters. Kelly went up to him with a warm smile and gave him a big hug. Blushing furiously,

Randall awkwardly hugged her back. Max heaved an inward sigh of deep relief.

A little while later he stretched out on the bed, arms behind his head, and watched her rehang her clothes. Deeply content, for once he didn't mind that she was crowding his pants and jackets into the nether regions of the closet.

"Even though I didn't win the Stonington, the nomination will no doubt result in more high-end work," he said. "I've been thinking, and I reckon it's time I leased offices in town and hired permanent help."

"That's an excellent idea," Kelly said, pinning a skirt to a hanger. "First thing tomorrow I'll go over our listings and see what's available. I know there's nothing in Hainesville at the moment, but there's this cute older house in Simcoe, near the center of town which you could convert into offices."

"I like the sound of an older house, something with character and style. I'll come in with you tomorrow and check it out." He paused. "You could take over my home office if you want. Or at least share it."

She cocked him a puzzled smile. "What would I need an office for?"

"To run your own real estate business from home?"

"Wouldn't work," she said, shaking her head. "Selling real estate relies on people walking past and seeing photos of the listings in the window." She took shoes from a plastic bag in her suitcase and placed them on the rack in her closet. "However," she added thoughtfully, "I might do something about turning my dried flowers into a business."

Max nodded. "That's an idea. People are always coming to you for dried flowers for crafts, or wanting you to make them arrangements. Why not cash in on your talent?"

"Randall was the one who suggested it initially," she explained. "At the time I wasn't inclined to listen to anything he said, but it could be a viable sideline."

"Or an alternative to real estate," Max suggested. When her expression hardened, he added, "You can't do everything, Kel. Please think about getting a cleaning lady in once or twice a week."

Kelly zipped up her empty suitcase and set it near the door, to be taken out to the garage. They were back at *that*. "I'm not going to pay for something I can do myself," she reiterated.

Frowning, Max said, "When will you stop trying to be a supermom?"

To his surprise, a look of sadness swept across her face. "I'm *not* a supermom." Then, before he could ask what she meant, her mood brightened. "Hey, when do you want to tell the kids we're renewing our vows?"

Max sprang off the bed. "Let's do it now."

KELLY AND MAX DECIDED to have the ceremony at home before the end of the month so Randall could be present. After the children got over their initial shock at their parents marrying again, they entered into preparations enthusiastically. Tina and Tammy were to be flower girls; they practiced strewing rose petals up an imaginary aisle so diligently that Kelly had to put a stop to it for fear there would be no roses left on the day. Beth took an interest in the menu and, under Kelly's supervision, made a list of food items, divided into what Kelly could make and what had to be bought. To Kelly's amusement, Robyn and Randall worked together on the invitations. Kelly assumed the invitations would be computer-generated; she was pleasantly surprised and touched when Randall hand-painted a design of their house entwined in a floral wreath and Robyn did the lettering with her calligraphy set. Then the pair got Max to take them to Simcoe to have the invitations printed.

When Kelly wasn't showing properties she went to work developing her dried-flower business. First she got Randall to show her the Internet Web sites he'd found, then she studied them for ideas. Next, she asked Erin to help her draw up a business plan. When she was confident the enterprise was viable on a small scale, she got Oliver, her stepniece Miranda's boyfriend, to photograph the different types of dried flowers and arrangements for inclusion in a print catalog and on the Web site Randall was designing for her.

On the rare occasions during all this frenetic activity when she paused to catch her breath, she experienced moments of panic at taking on too much. As a mother of four, one job was plenty, but two? And what if she ended up a mother of five? When her heart started to palpitate with anxiety and she got that sick feeling in her stomach she would get up and push on, not allowing herself to dwell on the what-ifs. Regarding her pregnancy, somehow everything had come to hinge on the ultrasound. When she had those results she would make decisions about the future. Until then, she was keeping her options open. And if, at the back of her mind, she was waiting to find out the baby's gender, she didn't like to admit it, not even to herself.

Max, meanwhile, took out a lease on the 1940s California bungalow on the edge of the business district in Simcoe. He contracted a builder to renovate and paid him to hire Randall as a sort of junior apprentice. Randall worked hard and willingly at any task set him and seemed as proud of the calluses forming on his hands as Max was of his efforts.

Two weeks before the ceremony, Kelly was in the kitchen when Max came home from work.

"How are the renovations going?" she asked, taking a tray out of the oven. Cooling on the counter were two dozen more miniquiches she'd made that afternoon to freeze for the reception.

"Excellent. I should be able to move in before the end of September." He looped an arm around her waist and pulled her away from the counter and into his embrace. "You look tired, honey. You're trying to do too much again. Why don't you ask your sisters to help with the food. I'm sure they'd be only too glad to bring something."

"They're busy, too, with family and work of their own," Kelly said. "Don't worry about me. I'll manage."

"If you say so." Max nuzzled her neck and slid his hands beneath her top. "I've been having this incredibly erotic fantasy about you all day. Come and I'll show you."

Kelly felt her body respond to his touch and pulled away. A few weeks ago she would have dragged him off to the bedroom. Now she avoided sex in case he noticed the changes in her breasts as a result of pregnancy. She pushed damp hair off her forehead. "I think I need to sit down for a bit."

Max frowned, studying her face. "Are you sure you're all right, Kel? You look a bit pale. Will you be up to Latin dancing tonight?"

Oh, God. She'd forgotten about the dance lessons. She was *so* tired, emotionally and physically stretched to her limits. But she smiled. "Of course. I'm fine."

"Want a glass of wine? I think there's a bottle of Australian chardonnay in the fridge."

"No, I can't." He glanced at her strangely and she patted her tummy, kicking herself for almost giving her condition away. "I...I've gained a couple of pounds lately. Got to watch my weight."

His disbelieving laughter rang in her ears. "You're on the go constantly. You've never had to watch your weight, even when you were pregnant. But never mind. I'll have a beer and get you some iced mineral water. Then we're going to go out on the patio and have a break." Before he moved off to the fridge, he kissed her on the cheek. "Let's have an early night."

Kelly nodded and turned the oven off. With a welcome cold drink in hand, she joined Max on the patio, where they watched Randall and the girls playing horseshoes. Randall was teasing Robyn over a wild throw and she was laughing good-naturedly, insisting she could still win.

"The kids get along great now, don't they?" Max said.

"They do," Kelly admitted.

Max took her hand, rubbing his thumb across her skin, and Kelly smiled, her heart full. While staying at Gran's, she'd missed family time even more than she'd expected. She was grateful beyond measure to be back with the people she loved.

"We're so lucky, Max, to have beautiful, healthy children." She blinked. "And each other."

"I know." His voice broke as he brought her hand to his lips. "Oh, sweetheart, don't I know."

Then Max glanced back to the children and a sigh lifted his chest. "I just wish Randall didn't have to leave. I feel we're all only just getting to know one another and in two weeks he'll be gone."

"He needs time with his parents before school starts." Kelly added gently, "This isn't his home."

"I realize that." Max sighed. "He's really changed since he's been here, though, hasn't he? More relaxed and confident, more his own person. And I swear he's grown over the summer. He's certainly built up the muscles in his arms. He's got a good eye, too. Look at how accurately he tossed that horseshoe.''

''He does look less like a computer nerd and more like a typical teenage boy,'' Kelly agreed. ''But there was nothing really wrong with him before he came here. It's not your duty, or even your right, to change him.''

''Of course. But it's been good for him to get to know the girls. I just wish my parents had taken an interest in him.''

''They're coming to the ceremony, aren't they?''

''Yeah.''

After that Max was silent so long she turned to look at him and was surprised to see his eyes full. ''Max, what is it?''

''I'm going to miss him, Kelly. I'm just plain going to miss him.''

''RENEWING YOUR VOWS is such a romantic idea,'' Geena said the next afternoon when she and Erin had dropped in for coffee. ''I'm so glad you and Max worked everything out.''

''Yeah,'' Kelly mumbled, ticking off items on her ''to do'' list. Invitations—check; clean house—the floors and bathrooms she would leave till the night before, but she could wash the windows this weekend. Quiches—check; sweet and sour meatballs—check. She'd made dozens of each—

"Kelly, hello?"

She glanced up. Erin was trying to get her attention. "Sorry. I'm a little distracted."

"I noticed. You don't have to do this all by yourself," Erin said. "Geena and I came over to see what we could do to help. Just let us know."

"Everyone would bring something if you asked," Geena said. "Edna Thompson is famous for her delicious sausage rolls and I would love to make a cake—"

The cake. She'd forgotten the cake! Kelly smiled brilliantly. "Thanks, but there's no need. I've got it all covered."

She would make the cake tonight, after the kids went to bed.…

"I was talking to Greta Vogler," Geena said, bouncing Sonja on her knee. "She saw the dried-flower arrangement you made me and wants one, too. She also has a friend in Tacoma who owns a craft shop and might be interested in placing an order."

"Fantastic. Tell Greta to call me. I'll get onto her arrangement right away." Kelly peered into the pantry, checking supplies and making a list of needed items for the wedding feast. "Randall's experiencing some glitches with the Web site, but maybe Friday after work I can get down to Tacoma with some samples for Greta's friend. Hopefully my catalog will be ready by then.''

Erin and Geena exchanged glances.

"Friday we're going shopping for your dress," Geena reminded her.

"I'm sure Greta and her friend can wait," Erin said. "You have enough on your plate."

Kelly handed Sonja a rusk. The baby girl turned round china-blue eyes on her and Kelly's heart constricted. Tomorrow was the ultrasound.

"I don't want to lose a potential customer." Kelly glanced frantically around the cluttered counters. "Where did I put my list. I need my list."

"Kelly!" Erin exclaimed. "You're driving yourself to a nervous breakdown."

"Here it is." Geena handed her a full page filled with single-spaced lines of tasks, about a third of which had been crossed off.

Kelly added Greta's flower arrangement to the bottom of the page. If only she had ten more hours in every day. No, make that twelve more hours.

"I'd better get going," Geena said, glancing at her watch. "It's nearly three."

"Three?" Kelly exclaimed. "It can't be!" She looked at the wall clock. "Oh, my God. I forgot to take Tina and Tammy to their swimming lesson at two-thirty.''

Her head was so crammed with things to remember it was going to explode. She'd had five hours' sleep last night and four hours the night before. Added to that was the crushing fatigue of early pregnancy. When the missed swimming lesson brought forth memories of Tina's fall into the river, Kelly's tenuous grip on control dissolved. Her face crumpled and she burst into tears.

''It's only one lesson,'' Erin said, alarmed. ''They'll make it up.''

''Kelly, sweetie, don't cry.'' Geena reached for her hand.

''I can't cope. It's too much,'' Kelly wailed. The strain and tension of the past weeks and months released in noisy gulping sobs. ''I'm a terrible mother. Terrible.''

''You're a wonderful mother,'' Erin protested, stroking her arm. ''You're my role model.''

''You're always so organized,'' Geena agreed. ''Somehow you're able to do everything—''

''I can't! No matter how much I do, I can never do enough!'' She heard the hysterical edge to her rising voice and was unable to contain it. ''I thought I could, but I can't. I'll end up neglecting it, or resenting it—''

"*It?* Kelly!" Erin took her by the shoulders and gave her a hard shake. "What are you talking about?"

Jolted into silence, Kelly blinked. Geena handed her a paper towel and Kelly blotted her tears. She dragged in a deep breath. "I'm pregnant."

Before her sisters could erupt with congratulations, she forestalled them. *"This isn't good news. I don't want this baby."*

Stunned into silence, Geena and Erin stared at her. Kelly closed her eyes in shame. How horrible was she not to want her own flesh and blood? Dr. Johnson had called her a natural mother, but there was nothing natural in the way she was feeling now.

"One night," she said bitterly. "One lousy night of lovemaking and I'm pregnant."

"That's all it takes," Geena said with a rueful smile. "I should know. It happened to me."

"Yes, but you *wanted* to have a baby. I don't." She paced away, pulling at her hair with both hands. "I'm going crazy trying to figure out how I'm going to fit everything in—Max and the girls, real estate, my new business—and now a baby. I…I don't see how I can do it all." She burst into tears again at having to admit that. She'd always been the one who could handle *anything*.

"What does Max say?" Erin asked.

"I haven't told him."

Erin and Geena digested this information in silence. Kelly knew they would conclude she was considering not telling him at all. Her heart was breaking under the strain of secrecy and the potential consequences to her marriage. This was a bigger secret than Lanni. Bigger even than Randall. It could tear her and Max apart forever.

Quietly, Erin and Geena came close, surrounding her with their arms, resting their heads on hers, enclosing her with their love. Kelly's heartache eased to a dull throb.

"I have to go in for an ultrasound tomorrow," she said. "All I can think of is, if I find out it's a boy, will that affect my decision?"

Her sisters hugged her tighter, feeling her pain. "No matter what you decide," Erin began, and Geena finished, "we'll be here for you. Always."

"Thanks." Tears spilled down Kelly's cheeks. "I love you."

CHAPTER THIRTEEN

"I HAVE TO DRIVE TO SEATTLE this morning to meet a client," Max said, draining the last of his orange juice. "Do you want to come with me and make contact with those craft stores you were talking about?" He knew she was taking a day off from the real estate office because she'd mentioned it at dinner the night before.

"This morning?" she said crossly. "I need more notice than *that*." She plunked a packed lunch down in front of him, shoved a hand through uncombed hair and closed her arms over her dressing gown.

Max winced as the paper sack hit the granite benchtop. "I hope there isn't an apple in there. I didn't make the arrangements until last night, and when I got to bed you were already asleep."

He was worried about her. For the past week she'd been in bed, asleep, before nine o'clock, only to rise in the night. Once he'd found her baking pastry shells for crab puffs at 2:00 a.m. Another time, he'd caught her folding laundry at midnight. "Do I take it the answer is no?"

"Of course it's no. My catalog still isn't printed and I've got so much to do around here it'll take me until next month to finish." She shuffled across the kitchen to return the milk to the fridge, still grumbling. "You could have told me you were driving to Seattle *before* I made you a sandwich."

"It won't go to waste. I'm meeting my client to discuss the concept design, then I'm coming home." He opened his briefcase and put the bag in, then stared as Kelly got the mop and bucket from the walk-in pantry and squirted floor cleaner into the bucket. "You're washing the floor now? I thought you had so much to do."

"This is one of the things I have to do. Anyway, what do you care when I wash the floor?" Kelly sloshed soapy water over the tiles with an urgency out of proportion to the task. "With five kids around, this place gets so dirty. Someone has to keep the house clean."

"You know we could fix that with one phone call to a cleaning lady." Max stepped carefully over the wet floor and took Kelly by the shoulders, forcing her to straighten. "Honey, what's wrong? You've been acting so strange lately."

Her eyes opened very wide. "Nothing's wrong. What could be wrong?"

He pulled her into a hug. "It's scary starting your own business. I was terrified when I first hung out my shingle and announced to the world I was an architect."

Her nose pressed to his suit jacket, she uttered a disbelieving snort of laughter that sounded suspiciously like a sob. "You were never scared."

"Sure I was. I just hid it." He stroked her hair, worried by her tears, which seemed to have sprung from nowhere. "You've been laying the foundations of this business for years without even knowing you were doing so. Why not give it your all and quit real estate?"

"Not until I'm sure I can make a go of it."

"You're going to be a huge success— I just know it."

"Thanks." Her lips curved briefly.

Her smile didn't reach her eyes, though, and that disturbed him. Where was his cheerful, carefree Kelly? "Is there anything else you want to tell me?"

Avoiding his gaze, she wiped her wet cheeks with the sleeve of her dressing gown. "You'd better go or you'll be late for your meeting."

"Okay," Max said, reluctant to leave her in this

odd emotional state. "I'll call you after my meeting, around lunchtime."

"No! I mean, I'll be out…you know, doing stuff."

Max picked up his briefcase and slowly backed away. "See you tonight, then. Take care. Love you."

She smiled brilliantly, fresh tears welling in her eyes. "Love you, too. Bye. I'm fine. *Go,* Max."

Max drove to Seattle, but his thoughts stayed in Hainesville, with Kelly. He didn't know what to make of her moods lately—one minute angry, the next weepy, and usually over nothing. Nothing that he could discern, anyway.

He met his client, Frank McMurtrie, on the fortieth floor of his office building and spent the morning going over Frank's requirements for a luxury penthouse apartment.

"How about lunch?" Frank suggested when they were done. "I found a great little seafood place near here."

Max opened his briefcase to stow his notebook full of detailed notes and measurements. The lunch Kelly had made him stared back accusingly. She hated wasting anything. With a shrug, he closed his briefcase. "Sounds good."

They walked from Frank's office building to the restaurant, a matter of only a few blocks. On the way, Max dialed home on his cell phone, even though

Kelly had told him not to. He'd counted twelve rings, when he suddenly stopped dead in the middle of an intersection and clicked off the phone. Kelly's station wagon was parked across the street, in front of the medical center.

"Something wrong, Max?" Frank asked from a few paces ahead when he'd noticed Max had stopped.

"No, nothing." The light turned and Max hurried to catch up, his gaze fixed on the car. Could he be mistaken? There were plenty of red Ford station wagons around. Coming closer, he saw Beth's baseball hat in the back window and a peeling bumper sticker that read Ballet Dancers Do It Gracefully. Robyn, thank goodness, had no apparent understanding of double entendre.

All through lunch, Max wondered and worried. Had Kelly changed her mind about contacting craft shops? Or did she have an appointment at the medical center? Her OB-GYN was in Everett, so if she was here for a medical visit it had to be for something other than a new IUD. The way she'd been acting all week suggested *something* was wrong with her.

Don't be ridiculous, he told himself. With all that had happened between them this summer he was stressed out and paranoid. Now that everything was starting to go well for them he was being foolish, imagining the worst. There had to be a simple explanation.

Nevertheless, a cold finger of fear traced his spine as he tried in vain to concentrate on what Frank was saying about the penthouse apartment. What if Kelly had some terrible disease?

But if that was true, why didn't she tell him?

Because she was Kelly. A pillar of strength. Supermom, who admitted no weakness and allowed nothing to stop her from taking care of her family.

Somehow he got through lunch, set another date with Frank for getting the concept design to him and headed for home via the northbound interstate freeway. His mind flip-flopped between worst-case scenarios and the impossibility of believing anything serious could be wrong with Kelly. He tried to call her again and again, but there was still no answer. When he pulled into the driveway and spotted her car parked outside the garage he breathed a sigh of relief. At least she was home.

''Where's your mother?'' he demanded of Beth, who was playing chess with Randall in the family room.

Beth glanced out the window and back at her father. ''In the garden.''

He found her in the sweet peas, waist-high in a

sea of fragrant purple, blue and pink petals and curling green tendrils. She grew these not for drying but because she loved the scent and the colors. A woven basket was slung over her arm and she was cutting flowers for the house. The sight of her slender figure and swinging hair glinting in the sun brought moisture to his eyes.

"Kelly!" He hurried over to her, striding through the rows of flowers, heedless of the damage he wreaked.

"Max!" She stared, aghast at the broken stalks and crushed flowers. "Slow down. What are you doing?"

He scooped her in his arms and pressed her to him, "My God, why didn't you tell me?"

She pulled back, stunned. "You know? How?"

"I saw your car parked outside the medical center." He framed her face with his hands. "You've got to trust me, Kelly. How bad is it?"

"*Bad?*" she repeated, clearly astonished. "I thought *you* at least would be happy."

"How can you say that? We've had our rough patches, but I love you. Even if I didn't, I'd never want anything awful to happen to you."

"Hold on," she said, frowning. "Just what do you think is wrong with me?"

"I don't know. Cancer?" He searched her face for reason to hope he was mistaken.

To his shock and amazement, she began to laugh.

"It's not funny," he said angrily. "I've been scared sick all afternoon." Her laughter continued, and with alarm he realized she was becoming hysterical. "*Kelly.* Snap out of it." He gave her a little shake.

All at once her laughter died and her eyes looked so old and tired he was afraid all over again. "For God's sake, Kelly. What is it?"

She stepped back from him, clutching her basket with both hands. "I'm pregnant."

For a moment all he could do was stare at her as his overwrought brain tried to take in the meaning of her words. Pregnant. *Pregnant.* They were going to have another baby! His heart lifted, bringing forth relieved, joyous laughter. "Oh, man, oh, Kelly. I thought…I thought you were dying and instead you're…" Unable to stop grinning, he threw up his hands in the effort to express his happiness. Tears again came to his eyes. "A baby." He held out his arms for her. "Come here, sweetheart."

Face frozen, she planted her feet and stayed put. "I don't want it."

He shook his head, his smile still in place. "But,

Kelly, it's our baby. I know you weren't keen on having more kids…still—''

She made another step back and her eyes took on a wild gleam. "I'm not having it."

At her obstinate tone his fist closed around a clump of sweet peas and with an abrupt movement he snapped off their heads. Kelly gasped at the deliberate destruction. Taking a deep breath to control his anger, he said, in the firm, calm voice that he used to settle the twins, "Why don't you start by telling me what you were doing at the medical center today. I take it you had a doctor's appointment?"

She nodded. "Dr. Johnson moved his clinic there. I went in for an ultrasound."

Max's thoughts flashed back to previous ultrasound images and his dawning feelings of love for their unborn children. Now he only felt a rush of anger toward Kelly for not letting him be present at the first sight of this new baby. He controlled that, too, with difficulty. She was obviously having a hard time with this pregnancy and it was up to him to help her through it.

"Let's sit down." He took her arm and led her out of the flower bed to a garden bench overlooking the river. Her gaze became fixed on the flowing water and he had to touch her shoulder to get her attention. "How far along are you?"

"Fourteen weeks."

The weekend at the Salish Lodge. Max experienced a stab of guilt, quickly followed by a purely male reaction—virility triumphant. He knew better than to let *that* show. "And the baby is fine?"

"What? Yes, it's fine."

"And are *you* okay?"

Head down, she nodded and mumbled something. "Pardon?"

Lifting her chin, she said, "They couldn't tell what sex it is."

As if that were his main concern. Although he guessed she could be forgiven for thinking it so, considering the attention he'd lavished on Randall all summer. "I don't care if it's a boy or girl."

"Sure you don't," she said bitterly.

Her hand lay inert in her lap so he laced his fingers through hers and rested their hands on his thigh. "Aren't you even a little bit happy, Kelly?"

Mutely, she shook her head.

"You feel down because this is so unexpected. Once you get used to the idea of having another baby, you'll feel differently—"

She shot to her feet, yanking her hand from his. "Don't patronize me. You don't have a clue how I feel. I'm telling you, Max, *I'm not having this baby.*"

Her threat struck fear in his heart as he rose to

confront her. "You can't make a unilateral decision. It's my baby, too."

"It's *my* body. *I'm* the one who has to carry it for nine months, and breast-feed it and care for it."

"You can't get rid of it because it doesn't fit in with your career plans."

"I didn't want another baby and you knew that," she said harshly. "Yet you conveniently forgot to bring condoms to the Salish Lodge."

"Birth control is a two-way responsibility. *You* happily made love without protection. You'd better not be suggesting I forgot on purpose."

"If the shoe fits…"

Suddenly he understood her behavior on his awards night. "You knew you were pregnant that night in Seattle. You've known for weeks!"

"So what if I have?"

They were face-to-face, shouting at each other in a scene uglier than any of their worst fights in the past.

"You've been stringing me along for years," he accused. "Promising me you'd consider another baby, while all the time you were lying. 'When the moment is right, when the twins are older,'" he mimicked her. "Maybe you didn't even want the twins."

Her face turned stark white. "How dare you!" she

gasped. "*You* only want more children so you can have a boy."

"*I do not!*"

She opened her mouth to shout back, but at his overloud denial she stopped and in a deadly calm voice said, "But, Max, you've already admitted to me you desperately want a boy. That's not a good-enough reason to have a baby. What if it's a girl? Maybe you wouldn't want it. Think of that poor child growing up knowing without having to be told that it wasn't wanted. That's worse than the mistake you made in conceiving Randall."

Max's vision blurred red. He hardly knew what he was saying. "The only mistake I made over Randall was giving him up for adoption in the first place. If I hadn't married you—"

Revelation dawned in her horror-stricken face. "You blame *me* for having to give up your son years ago."

"No!" He shook his head vehemently. "That's not true. It's not." He backed away as present anger confused past emotions, mixing things up in his mind.

"Of course it is," she insisted. "If I hadn't been in the picture you probably would have married Lanni and kept Randall. Now you're angry because I won't give you another chance at a son all your own.'' She brandished her secateurs. ''*That's* what's been bothering me all along about having another baby. It wasn't so much the idea of giving up work, although I really did want a chance at my own life for a change. No, it's the feeling I'm being blackmailed into getting pregnant because I owe you.'' Tears puddled in her eyes, and her chest heaved several times before she gained enough breath to speak. ''It's over between us, Max. And you can forget about me having this baby. I won't bring a child into a dysfunctional relationship.''

''You're damn right this marriage is over,'' he shouted, ''if you could even *think* about aborting our child.''

Max stalked back to the house, leaving Kelly alone by the river. This wasn't the woman he'd fallen in love with, the woman he'd defied his parents and turned his back on his only son to be with. She was *wrong,* wrong about everything.

Striding through the family room, he ignored Beth and Randall's worried looks and went to his office. At the door he stopped short, surveying the stacks of gardening books and flower presses Kelly had brought in to replace his things. Fuming, he waded through to his chair.

Moments later he heard footsteps in the hall and

got up, to see Kelly putting on her shoes, a suitcase on the floor at her feet. "Running away again?"

She ignored him.

So be it. This time when she walked out the door he didn't try to stop her.

"I DON'T UNDERSTAND what happened," Robyn fretted, slumping her ordinarily straight back in a chair. The five children had met in Beth's room for an emergency conference. "After they came back from Dad's awards night they were so happy." She turned to Randall. "Did Dad say anything to you about why she left?"

Randall shook his head. He was worried, too, although a small part of him was pleased Robyn had referred to *her* father as *his* father. Her acceptance went a long way to easing the tightness in his chest. At least this time she wasn't blaming him for her mother's departure.

Beth's legs dangled from the top bunk as she twisted her baseball cap in her hands. "They're supposed to be getting married again. Do you think they'll still go through with the ceremony?"

"I overheard Max on the phone telling someone it was canceled," Randall replied.

"Well, I don't think he got through to everyone," Robyn put in. "Mabel Gribble phoned today and asked if we wanted to borrow chairs from the town hall. I didn't know what to tell her.''

"What *did* you say?'' Randall asked, racking his brains for answers. There had to be *something* they could do to fix Max and Kelly's marriage.

"I said I'd ask Mom.'' She glanced at her watch. "I wonder if she'll come back tonight for dinner.''

"Uh-uh,'' Beth said. "Dad said he was going to make us pizza. It sounded like he didn't *want* her to come home,'' she added miserably.

Robyn shook her head. "This is bad.''

Tammy wailed, "Me and Tina want to be flower girls.''

"Flower fairy princesses,'' Tina corrected, reaching for Tammy's hand to comfort her.

"We can't let them call off the wedding.'' Randall thumped a fist on his knee. "If Max and your mom are too upset to finish the arrangements, then it's up to us to make sure they renew their vows.''

"We're just kids,'' Beth protested. "Besides, they don't *want* to be married anymore. They're more likely to get divorced, instead.''

"They had a big fight before and got over it, didn't they?'' Randall argued.

"Yes, but this is different,'' Robyn said. "I've never seen Dad this angry and if Mom's not even coming home to fix dinner…''

"We have to think positive," Randall declared. "Imagine how disappointed they'd be if they did make up but couldn't renew their vows because nothing was prepared. What did that guy say in that old video we watched the other day? 'Build it and they will come'?"

"He was talking about a baseball diamond," Robyn said scornfully. "Besides, that was a fantasy."

"Doesn't matter," Randall maintained. "What he meant was, if you believe in something, you can make it happen."

"Do you really believe that?" Beth asked, perking up a little.

"Sure," Randall said. "I believed my biological father was a really great guy, and he is. I believed he'd want to know me as much as I wanted to know him, and he did."

"Wow," Beth said. "I guess you're right."

Robyn took a little longer to consider the notion, but eventually she, too, nodded. "Mom's always talking about the power of positive thinking." She smiled, her forehead clearing. "Who knows? It's just crazy enough to work."

Randall breathed out in relief. He wouldn't tell Robyn and Beth that he'd believed equally in Lanni and she'd let him down; they were a little young to be exposed to the hard facts of life. Besides, Kelly was different from Lanni. She really loved Max. And she loved her children. He couldn't believe she'd do anything to hurt her family.

"First thing we have to do is tell everyone the wedding is still on," Randall said. "Robyn, can you do that?"

Robyn sat up tall and straight. "Of course. I've still got the list Mom gave me when we were sending out the invitations. While I'm at it, I'll swear them to secrecy."

"Great. And Beth, can you get a handle on the food?"

"No sweat." Beth jammed her cap on her head over her springy hair and swung down off the top bunk, ready to go to work immediately. "Most of it's done and in the freezer. I can make a list of what else we need— But how are we going to get the groceries?"

"Why don't we ask everyone to bring something?" Robyn suggested. "That's what Janie's mom does when their family gets together."

"Mom doesn't believe in pot luck," Beth said. "She likes to do it all herself."

"Tough," Robyn said ruthlessly. "She's not organizing this anymore—we are."

"Right," Randall agreed. "It would help if we

had an adult working with us, though. Do you think we could ask your Gran?''

''Definitely,'' Robyn said. ''What about the music? I think Mom was going to ask Mabel Gribble to play the piano.''

''And we can pick flowers from the garden for Mom's bouquet,'' Beth suggested.

''Tina and me'll get rose petals,'' Tammy piped up.

''Good girls.'' Randall rose. ''I'll confirm the date with the minister and make sure Max doesn't miss his own wedding.''

''But how are we going to get Mom to come?'' Beth said.

Randall was stumped for a moment, then his face lit. ''She'll come home if her kids ask for her. How are you at faking being sick?''

Beth flapped a hand. ''Piece of cake.''

CHAPTER FOURTEEN

"ARE YOU SURE YOU'RE doing the right thing, Kelly?" Gran stood on the front porch of her house, pleading with her granddaughter.

Kelly, on the bottom step, gazed down the street. Erin and Geena would arrive any moment to take her to the Planned Parenthood clinic for a medical termination.

"I'm doing the only thing I *can* do, Gran." Beneath her tank top and cotton skirt she was perspiring lightly in the exceptional heat. "Believe me, I'm not happy about this, but everything's such a mess."

Have the baby. Don't have the baby. The more she rationalized she was doing the right thing, the more her gut was telling her it was a mistake.

"But this is so...final." Gran twisted her hands in her apron. "Take another day to think about it."

Stubbornly, Kelly shook her head. She'd been doing nothing *but* for a whole week. During that time, Max hadn't once called, nor had she been home; she missed her family desperately.

Gran tried again. "Have you talked it over with Max?"

"Max and I are past talking. Yesterday I was in town and saw him going into Bill Hayes' office."

There were two lawyers in town: Richard Wyman, whom Max used for his business and corporate dealings; and Bill Hayes, a family lawyer who specialized in divorce and custody settlements.

"Oh," said Gran, clearly drawing the same conclusion Kelly had. She smoothed down her apron with both hands. "I wasn't supposed to tell you this...the children made me promise to keep their secret, but..."

"But what?"

"They're proceeding with plans for the ceremony to renew your vows. They think if they make it happen you and Max will have to recommit to each other."

Kelly threw up her hands in disbelief. "Gran! How could you encourage them in such a crazy scheme? Going through the motions won't fix my marriage."

"I know that. They're hoping, as we all are, that you and Max will come to your senses in time." Gran smiled hopefully. "You could give it a try, if only to save the embarrassment of having the whole town show up at your house, to find there's no wedding."

"Oh, God. Another thing to worry about. Look, they'll never be able to organize it. Surely people will realize. Max is probably fielding phone calls right now, telling folks nothing's going to happen. I'll drive over there later and make sure. Right now—"

Erin's car pulled up at the curb. Geena got out the passenger side and waved.

Kelly waved back to show she'd seen them, then ran up the steps to hug her grandmother. "Don't hate me, Gran."

Gran's arms closed around her. "Don't be silly, child. I could never hate you. I just want you to be sure this is really best for you. As always, I trust your judgment."

Kelly hurried to Erin's car and opened the back door. Baby Sonja and little Erik turned her way simultaneously with welcoming smiles, giving Kelly a severe jolt to her heart.

"For crying out loud," she groaned. "An abortion clinic is no place to take babies."

"They're not coming," Geena hastened to assure her, releasing Sonja's car seat as she spoke. "Gran will watch them until we get back."

Thank God. If she had to look at those innocent faces all the way to the clinic she'd never be able to go through with the procedure. Erin came around to get Erik out and grabbed a tote bag filled with bottles, diapers and toys. Kelly waited impatiently while they took the children inside.

Within fifteen minutes they were on the interstate heading south and Kelly was wishing she were anywhere but in that car. Erin and Geena had attempted to engage her in conversation but when she made it clear she didn't feel like talking they chatted quietly in the front seat, comparing notes on their babies. Kelly tried not to listen. They weren't being insensitive, they were simply absorbed with the daily care and activities of their children.

She was doing the right thing. She had to believe that.

Erin slowed to turn onto the street where the Planned Parenthood clinic was located. Outside the clinic a small knot of protesters had gathered, some of them holding placards.

"Oh, no," Geena muttered. "I was afraid of this."

"Don't worry, Kel, we'll be right beside you," Erin assured her.

Even so, Kelly was trembling as she started up the walk to the clinic's front door accompanied by shouts and jeers. Erin and Geena flanked her, their arms around her waist, providing physical as well as moral support. A scowling elderly man thrust a placard in her face that read Baby Killer. Kelly recoiled, thrusting a hand up to shield her eyes.

Erin tightened her grip on Kelly's arm. "Don't let them get to you."

"I'm fine," Kelly said, feeling sick inside. She had a right to choose...but had she made the right choice?

Geena went ahead to hold open the door. "We're here."

Kelly filled out a form with her medical details, then sat in the waiting room, flipping through a magazine to take her mind off what was ahead. At last a nurse appeared in the doorway and called, "Kelly Walker?"

"Coming." She rose and hugged Erin and then Geena. "I...I'll see you after."

"We'll be here," Erin assured her. "Take care, Kel."

Geena gave her an extra squeeze. "Everything's going to be okay."

Kelly was shown into a cubicle and given a hospital gown to change into. Then she sat and waited some more, her bare toes curled on the carpeted floor, her knees pressed together. The longer she sat there, the worse she felt. As hard as she tried not to think of the baby she was carrying, she couldn't help wondering what he or she might have turned out like.

A little late now, she told herself fiercely, and tried to focus, instead, on which flowers she would plant next year. Larkspur, marigolds, baby's breath—

Damn. Where was that nurse? Why was this taking so long? She wiped her eyes. Then leaned against the wall with her head back and started to count the tiny holes in the ceiling tiles. After the third row she lost track and gave up.

Rummaging in her purse for a piece of gum, she came across a slip of flimsy paper. The ultrasound image of the baby. Oh, God. Why hadn't she thrown that away? She crumpled the paper, but the image wouldn't leave her mind.

It didn't seem that long ago that she'd been pregnant with Robyn. At the time, her friends had told her her life was over, that her marriage wouldn't last, that she'd end up a single mom before she was twenty. What did they know? She and Max had doted on each other and on Robyn. While they'd had their ups and downs as a couple, they'd stayed together thirteen years, and despite the awful things said during their last fight, she was still in love with him.

He'd loved her, too, until she decided to terminate this pregnancy.

When Beth had come along Kelly had worried she wouldn't have the capacity to love two children as much as one. She could smile at her ignorance. Love expanded—infinitely, it seemed. It was a law of the universe. Beth had turned out to be a completely different person from Robyn, but she was no less loved.

Tammy and Tina hadn't been planned and Kelly remembered her anxiety when she'd found out she was pregnant—and with twins! She'd just signed up for part-time college studies and had had to drop out. Funny, now she couldn't imagine life without her mischievous little angels. All her children had enriched her beyond measure. They gave meaning to her marriage and purpose to her life. Even Randall. He wasn't hers, but she'd come to accept him all the same.

Kelly's smile faded. Yes, she'd overcome hurdles with each of her other children. But this pregnancy was different. Now she knew about Lanni and Randall. And just how badly Max wanted a boy.

Despite their love, she and Max had too many issues without bringing the stresses and strains of a new baby into their lives.

Almost fearfully, she flattened the crumpled ultrasound image against her knee. That blurry peanut body with the overlarge head was her baby.

What did *she* want?

Deep inside, emotion welled, spilling over in tears.

Not from guilt, but regret. She would never hold this child. Never feel her little arms around her neck or exclaim over her first steps. Never experience her budding personality or watch her grow to adulthood. *Nev-er, nev-er, nev-er.* Kelly's heartbeat seemed to thump out the word over and over. She knew she would grieve this baby's loss for the rest of her life.

Footsteps approached. Kelly dabbed her eyes as a young nurse drew back the curtain. "Mrs. Walker?" she said. "It's time."

MAX POSITIONED THE SPRINKLER next to Kelly's sweet peas and turned on the tap, watching the spray as it arced up and over, making sure the entire garden bed received water. If Kelly was going to have a harvest she couldn't neglect her plants the way she did her family.

He wiped the sweat from the back of his neck with a handkerchief. The painful memory of their last fight hung over him. He wished he could delete *it* from his memory, or at least take back those ugly words. All their expectations and frustrations had been laid bare, leaving their feelings for each other as naked as a newborn. And just as vulnerable.

If she truly wanted to be free, if she couldn't be happy with him as he was, he would let her go. It was as simple, and as complex, as that. Even though everything in him rebelled against the thought of parting.

Max dried his hands on his jeans and walked back inside. The house was quiet. Where were the kids? All week they'd been closeted in Beth's bedroom or running out of the house on mysterious errands. So far they'd been surprisingly philosophical about their mother's most recent departure. For the moment he was avoiding telling them the truth: that her absence—or his—could well be permanent.

He popped the top on a cold beer and chugged half of it down in one gulp. For the hundredth time that afternoon he glanced at his watch. She must be back from the clinic by now, recuperating at her grandmother's house. He should call her. His intense grief and anger over what she'd done warred with his guilt over driving her to it. Yet how could he not make contact when he knew she, too, must be hurting?

The cordless phone wasn't in its socket. He pressed the search button and followed the beeping down the hall. It was coming from Beth's bedroom. As he approached, Tina ran out of her room, stopped dead when she saw him, then raced to Beth's room. She knocked once, went in and slammed the door.

"Don't slam the door," Max called out. "How many times— Oh, forget it."

He came abreast of Beth's room and heard the mingled voices of five children. What on earth were they up to? He knocked on Beth's door and started to turn the knob.

"Don't open the door!" Robyn shrieked. A body slammed against the door, shutting it in his face.

"Are you changing?" What was he saying? Randall was in there. "I need the phone. Have you got it?"

Silence met his question. Then Beth said, "Can't you use your mobile?"

"Not when I'm at home and there's a perfectly good land line available."

The door opened and Robyn handed over the phone. "We're expecting a call back, so could you hurry, please?"

"I'll do my best. Ma'am." He took the phone to his office. *Kelly's* office. Whatever. He settled in his chair and was about to dial Ruth's number, when the phone rang. "Hello, Kelly?" he said hopefully.

"No, it's Mabel Gribble. Is that you, Max?"

"Yes. Kelly isn't home right now. Could I get her to call you back?" What did the mayor's wife want with Kelly? Unless she was phoning about Sunday and hadn't heard the ceremony was canceled.

"I was returning Robyn's call," Mabel said. "May I speak with her?"

"*Robyn?*" Now, that was *very* odd. "I'll get her." As Max started back down the hall, he said to Mabel, "You did hear about the change of plans regarding our renewal of vows…?"

"Oh, I heard all right," Mabel said coyly, leaving Max thinking the gossips must be having a field day with his and Kelly's split, until she gushed, "I just *love* weddings. And a renewal of vows is even more romantic."

He knocked on Robyn's door. It was opened instantly by Randall. "But, Mabel, I don't think you understand," Max went on. "Kelly and I *aren't*—"

Tina reached up and snatched the phone from his hand before he could finish his sentence. "Thanks, Daddy." She smiled sweetly and shut the door in his face.

"Tina!" He was about to open the door and teach her some manners, when he heard the dogs making a commotion out back. What now? He walked through the house and onto the patio to investigate.

Kelly, her back to him, was shifting the sprinkler to another site, as Billy and Flora barked gleefully and leaped around their mistress. Max shoved a hand through his hair. She must have walked around the side of the house straight to the flower bed, and what with talking to Mabel and the kids, he'd missed hearing her car pull up.

The sprinkler in place, she sank to her knees in the damp grass and put her arms around the dogs' necks while they licked her face—something she normally never allowed. He was about to call her name, when he realized by the slump of her shoulders that she was crying.

He ought to feel righteous satisfaction at her unhappiness—she'd made the choice; she would suffer for it. But all he felt was an overwhelming longing to comfort her. As much as he might want to hate her, the hell of it was, he still loved her. He always would.

She didn't look up at his approach. Possibly she didn't even hear his silent footfalls across the damp grass, locked as she was in her own grieving. His touch on her shoulder made her glance up, and his heart contracted at the sight of her cheeks wet with tears and the lines of suffering on her face.

"I'm sorry, Max," she said. "I'm so sorry."

Whatever anger was left in his heart dissolved. Crouching, he drew her into his arms and pulled her head down on his shoulder. "Shh, love. Everything's going to be all right."

She clung to him. "Max, please don't leave me. I love you."

He nodded, unable to speak, and held her closer. He pictured a baby girl—the only sort he knew—lost and gone forever. Tears spilled from his eyes and fell in Kelly's hair. "You shouldn't be up and about," he said at last, drawing back. "Come. You should be in bed."

A deep sigh ran through her and she wiped her eyes with the heel of her hand. "I didn't do it, Max."

She spoke so quietly he wasn't sure he'd heard correctly. "What did you say?"

Clearing her throat, she gave him a tentative smile. "I couldn't go through with it. I'm still pregnant. We're going to have a baby."

FOR THE THIRD TIME that afternoon, there was an unexpected knock at Beth's bedroom door.

"Quick, hide everything," Randall urged the girls in a whisper, then called out, "Be right there."

Robyn shuffled sheets of paper into a desk drawer while Beth helped Tina and Tammy roll up the banner they'd made—which read: Congratulations, Kelly And Max—and shove it under the bed. Randall had generated the lettering on the computer and the twins had colored it in with magic markers and plenty of sparkles. Preparations for the ceremony were complete; now all they had to do was get Mrs. Walker to show up.

The knock came again. "Open up, kids," Max ordered.

Randall gave the room a final quick check, and the girls hurried back to their seats to pose, innocent as angels. All except Beth, who positioned herself lying on the bunk bed, a hand draped melodramatically over her forehead.

Randall opened the door.

Kelly was standing next to Max. Her face was stained with tears, but she was smiling and she and Max had their arms around each other.

Max cleared his throat. "We, uh, just wanted to let you all know that your mom is home to stay and—"

He got no further as the children interrupted with a loud chorus of cheers. Max looked at Kelly and smiled.

"Ahem!" he said loudly. "We have more good news."

The girls quieted immediately. Randall anticipated an announcement about reinstating the ceremony and hid his excitement, relishing the surprise on their faces when they found out what he and the others had accomplished.

"Let me tell them," Kelly implored her husband. Her gaze went to each of her daughters in turn before resting on Randall. Then her smile widened to encompass them all in her announcement. "We're going to have another baby."

There was a moment's stunned silence, then Robyn leaped off the bed to embrace her mother. "Oh, Mom, that's wonderful."

"Cool!" Beth exclaimed, abandoning her sick bed to follow suit. The twins clamored for a hug, too.

Amid the exclamations and hugs, Max caught Randall's eye and winked. Randall swallowed and smiled back. He was due to go home tomorrow, after the ceremony. With a new baby on the way, would Max forget about him?

Randall pushed the thought from his mind and put out his hand to add his congratulations. Max took it and clapped him on the back.

"Oh, don't be so formal." Kelly nudged Max aside and pulled Randall into a hug.

Max and Kelly went out of the room soon after, leaving the children delighted by the unexpected turn of events.

Randall took off his glasses and polished them on his shirt, more relieved than smug. "Didn't I tell you if we 'built it' they would come?"

Robyn shook her head in amazement. "I can't believe they're back together. And in the nick of time."

"We should have told them about the ceremony," Beth said.

Randall looked to Robyn, who said, "They've got plenty to think about without worrying about tomorrow."

"I agree," Randall said. "Let's surprise them."

CHAPTER FIFTEEN

KELLY HAD A SHOWER, put on her sexiest satin-and-lace nightgown and slid into bed beside Max. "Hello, stranger."

Max's appreciation shone in his eyes as he reached for her. "Stranger, huh? I can't wait to get acquainted."

Like sunlight on water, warm loving feelings shimmered through Kelly as Max kissed her and stroked her. She'd missed him so badly. He'd missed her, too, by the feel of things.

She broke away to ask, "So will you call Bill Hayes on Monday and stop proceedings?"

Max rose on his elbow to slide a strap over her shoulder and kiss the skin beneath. "How did you know I went to see Bill?"

"I was on my way to the bank when I saw you go into his office." Her mouth tugged downward at the memory of her hurt. Maybe this wasn't the best time to raise the subject, but talking it out was better than worrying in isolation. "You must have been really mad at me to file for divorce so quickly. Are you sure you're ready to get back together?''

Max drew back, eyebrows raised. "Divorce?" His slight smile showed a mixture of tenderness and regret. "Is that what you thought? Oh, Kelly."

"What was it, if not that?"

"I was changing my will to include Randall."

"Oh, my God!" Kelly flopped on her back, hand on her heart. "Good grief, Max. The only reason I got as far as the abortion clinic was that I thought you were ending our marriage."

"I would have told you before I did anything so drastic as file for divorce."

She sighed and gave him a quick smile. "Yeah, well, I guess I was pretty upset and confused."

"That makes two of us." Max spread his hand across the gentle curve of her belly, as though keeping the baby inside safe from harm. "What made you change your mind?"

She turned to him, eyes shining. "I realized I want this baby, not to please you but for myself. Then I remembered what you said about making our love bigger when times are tough, and everything seemed to fall into place. Who I am doesn't depend on what I do, but who I love. And who loves me." She sighed. "After I die no one will care whether I sold a million houses or ran a successful business. But hopefully my children and grandchildren will think of me and remember I loved them.'' She put her hand on top of his on her belly. ''Already I love this baby. Part of the strain was trying to deny that.''

Max kissed Kelly lightly. ''She'll be beautiful, just like her mom.''

Kelly smiled, hugging her secret to her. ''What did you leave Randall in your will?''

''His parents are well off so I didn't think it appropriate that I leave him money, especially when we have enough children to divide the pie among already. I wanted him to have something of his heritage, so I left him one of the model ships my grandfather built. Do you think the girls will mind?''

''They'll understand. I think it's a lovely gesture.'' She snuggled beneath the covers, seeking his warmth.

Max slid down, too, running his hands over her hips to pull her in close. ''I'm sorry your dried-flower thing isn't going to work out.''

''Oh, I'm not giving that up.'' Kelly wriggled her pelvis up against his.

''Kelly,'' he said, a warning note in his voice. ''You can't run yourself ragged, not when you're pregnant. You've got to accept some help.''

She smiled. ''I fully intend to.''

"You do?" He looked at her with some astonishment.

"While I was sorting out my priorities, I came to the conclusion that people can't do everything, so they might as well do what they love. In my case, that's my family and my flowers. I'm going to quit real estate and take you up on your offer of a cleaning lady a couple days a week."

"Hallelujah." He rolled his eyes to the heavens, then narrowed his gaze on her. "As long as you don't clean in preparation for the cleaning lady."

"If I do, I give you permission to lock my broom closet..." She trailed off, distracted because Max was doing what *he* loved to do and that was touching her. Putting a hand on his chest, she said, "Before we get completely carried away, are we all sorted out?"

Max stopped to consider. "I think so. Before, we were too caught up in the emotional aspects of the problem to think clearly."

"Don't knock emotion," she said. "It's the glue that holds us together."

"Amen to that. *Now* are we done talking?" Max shifted her beneath him. "Because I'm about to make love to you."

She opened her mouth to say she was ready, but

never got the words out; apparently his question was rhetorical.

THE NEXT MORNING MAX was awakened by the sound of someone pounding on the door.

Sitting up in bed, he growled, "Where's the fire?"

"Do you know what time it is?" Robyn called.

He glanced over Kelly's shoulder at the clock. "Eleven-fifteen."

"Get *up,* or you'll be late," Beth joined in.

"What for? It's Sunday."

"It's your wedding day," Randall's voice added.

Was the whole family out there? And were they all demented? "We canceled, remember?"

"We called everyone up and told them it was on again," Randall said.

"You didn't!"

"We did."

Beside him, Kelly moaned and covered her face. "I forgot all about that."

Max turned to stare at her. "You knew about this?"

"Only after the fact."

The door opened and the five children entered the bedroom, clustering for mutual support.

"Everything's prepared, Dad," Robyn said. "You and Mom are just going to have to show up and go through with it. You wouldn't want to disappoint the whole town, would you?''

She sounded so sure of herself Max didn't know whether to applaud her or ground her for a month. "When did you get to be the lady of the house, issuing orders?" He turned to his son. "Randall, why didn't you stop them?"

Beth grinned. "It was his idea."

Tina ran to her father and tugged on the blankets. "Get up and get dressed, Daddy. You, too, Mommy. It starts in an hour."

Max turned to Kelly, still rumpled with sleep. "Looks like everyone's counting on this to go ahead. How about it? Will you marry me?"

She smiled and rolled her eyes. "I guess we can't disappoint the children. But the food, the music—"

"*Everything* is taken care of," Robyn said firmly. "It might not be done exactly the way you would do it, but we can handle more than you think. You're not indispensable, you know."

Tammy threw her arms around Kelly's neck. "Except for hugs."

"Thank God for that." Kelly's arms closed around her daughter.

Shortly before the ceremony was to start, Max knocked on Randall's door. The guests were being shown to chairs set out on the lawn outside the living room, where Mabel Gribble's piano playing could be heard through the open French doors. Marcus and Audrey Tipton had come for the party and would take Randall home with them when they left. Max wanted a few minutes alone with his son before that happened.

"Come in," Randall called, and Max entered, holding a model of the trawler his grandfather had fished from for thirty years off the Pacific Northwest.

Randall's suitcase was open on the bed, his computer already in boxes. When he saw Max he put down the books he was packing.

Max suddenly found it hard to speak. Clearing his throat, he thrust forward the model ship. "I was going to leave this to you in my will, then I thought, why wait? I'd like you to have it now."

Randall took the boat, his eyes moist behind his glasses. "Th-thank you. I don't know what to say."

"You don't have to say anything. I'm really glad we've had this time together, Randall. It's been very special."

Randall nodded, swallowing. "For me, too. I...I guess now that you're going to have a new baby..." He trailed off, looking profoundly uncomfortable.

Max frowned. "What about the baby?"

Randall took in a deep breath. "If it's a boy, you...you won't need me anymore."

Max went extremely still, as if his very cells had frozen. He was horrified that Randall even thought it might be true. *Was* it? Max gazed at the boy before him—his nerdy glasses, his endearing freckled skin, his intelligent, anxious gaze. Suddenly, with startling clarity, Max understood, not just theoretically, but in his heart, what having a son really meant to him.

"No, Randall!" he exclaimed. "I don't love you because you're some generic male offspring. If I had *fifty* sons I'd still want *you,* just because you're, well, *you.*" He lifted his hands in a gesture of helplessness, not sure he'd explained anything at all. "As far as I'm concerned, this is only the beginning of a life-long relationship. We want you to visit us as often as you can. And we'll come to see you...." Max opened his outstretched arms. "Okay?"

Randall gulped and bobbed his head. "Okay." Then he set the ship on Robyn's desk and stumbled into Max's embrace.

"Max?" a female voice called from the hallway.

Releasing his son with a watery smile, Max turned to the man and woman who'd appeared in the door-way. "Mom? Dad? I'd like you to meet my son. This is Randall."

"How do you do, Randall," said Elsa Walker, ex-tending her hand. Her blond hair was freshly styled and she wore a pale blue dress. Noticing the model ship on the desk, she said, "My father-in-law made that. You resemble him a little about the jaw. Don't you think so, Barry?"

Barry Walker, uncomfortably hot in a dark suit, shrugged and might have remained silent until Max leveled him a hard glance. Then he responded with a gruff, "More in the eyes, I'd say."

"He looks like himself," Max said. "You know, I think I hear Kelly calling us." He put an arm around Randall's shoulders. The boy relaxed a little as the elder Walkers moved off down the hall. "Give them a bit of time. They'll loosen up."

He made sure his parents found a seat, then went in search of Kelly.

"Where've you been?" she demanded anxiously. "We're just about ready to start."

"I've never seen you more beautiful," he said, admiring the simple lines of her ivory linen dress. Baby's breath adorned her shining hair, which hung loose to her shoulders. He'd enjoyed the exotic stranger of the hotel room, but the woman he wanted to live out his days with was his own familiar Kelly.

Inside, Mabel Gribble played the opening chords of the song they'd chosen—their signal to begin the procession down the aisle. Instead of going singly, they were to walk together, a symbol of their path through life.

Ignoring the music, Kelly took his hands in hers and said in a low, serious voice, "Max, I had another ultrasound at the Planned Parenthood clinic. I know the baby's gender."

"Why are you telling me now?" He glanced toward the assembled guests, who were all gazing curiously at them.

"I thought you'd want to know."

Max smiled into Kelly's eyes. "Thanks, but it doesn't matter anymore."

Then he tucked her arm into his and began the walk up the aisle. Tina and Tammy went before them, strewing geranium petals because they'd run out of rose petals. Robyn and Beth followed behind, holding miniature bouquets. Randall brought up the rear.

"But Max—"

"I mean it, Kel. It's no longer important to me whether the baby is a boy or a girl. Boys and girls are individuals and I love them equally."

"But what about carrying on the Walker family name? You have no brothers."

"I have two male cousins. Besides, Robyn tells me she's going to keep her maiden name when she marries and pass it on to her children."

"Max, she's twelve years old! She could easily change her mind."

"I'm no longer concerned about the family name, Kelly." He lifted her bouquet to his nose and quoted, 'A rose by any other name would smell as sweet.'"

They came to a halt in front of the minister, who smiled in greeting, then frowned mildly as they continued their conversation.

"But Max—"

"I'm telling you, it doesn't matter whether I have a son to raise or not. After four beautiful girls, how could I be unhappy with another daughter?"

Kelly searched his face and finally seemed to accept that he truly meant it. "Max, this means the world to me."

He took both her hands in his. "Promise you'll never run away again?"

"Never," she said softly. "I'm yours forever."

"That's all I wanted to know."

The minister cleared his throat. "'Dearly beloved—'"

Frowning, Kelly gave her bouquet a frustrated shake. "I can't stand you not knowing. I'm going to tell you...anyway."

"Nope." Max shook his head. "Don't want to know."

"I can't keep this a secret for five more months." Kelly protested.

The assembled guests began to fidget and murmur

among themselves. The minister cleared his throat again and adjusted his open prayer book with an elaborate movement.

"Let's get on with the ceremony," Max suggested. "Everyone's waiting."

But Kelly couldn't drop it. "I can't believe you don't want to know."

"Surprise me." He turned to face the minister. "'Dearly beloved—'"

"If it's a surprise, how can we plan ahead?" Kelly argued in an urgent whisper. To the minister she said, "We'll just be a minute here." To Max, she went on, "I won't be able to buy anything gender related. Everything will have to be yellow or green." She tugged on his sleeve. "I've never noticed this maddening lack of curiosity in you before, and I've got to say, it's not an attractive quality. I don't care if you don't want to know, I'm going to tell you, anyway. The baby is a—"

Robyn, Beth, Tina and Tammy, lined up to Kelly's right, exchanged wide-eyed glances, then leaned in to listen. Randall, on Max's left, did the same.

Max did the only thing he could do to shut her up; he kissed her.

Mabel Gribble, looking through the window and thinking the ceremony was over, struck up the wedding march. The audience hesitated, then broke into applause.

Pulling back, Kelly laughed and threw up her hands. "I give up. If you don't want to know, I won't tell you."

Their daughters slumped a little, disappointed.

Max breathed a sigh of relief. "*Now* can we get on with the ceremony?"

Kelly shot him a look of exasperated, indulgent love. "Do we really need to? We've already spoken the most important words in our lives to each other."

"True." Max glanced at the audience, who watched, puzzled but patient. Mabel had stopped playing again. "On the other hand, our friends and family expect a show and the kids have worked hard to get things ready."

"You're right." Kelly turned to the minister. "Please proceed."

Completely discombobulated, the minister once again intoned, "'Dearly beloved,'" then stopped and eyed Max and Kelly warily, as if to see whether they were going to start another discussion. When they faced him attentively, he took a deep breath and continued with the ceremony.

At last they'd said their "I do's" and walked down the aisle amid a chorus of cheers and Mabel's renewed efforts on the piano. As they reached the end of the aisle and the crowd rose to surge around them, Robyn tugged on her mother's dress. "Mom! *I* want to know."

Beth, Tina and Tammy crowded around. "We want to know, too," Beth said. Randall stood a little apart, but Kelly could tell he was just as interested.

Kelly glanced at Max, who was being borne off by Nick and Ben. She waved Randall over to join their little group. "Can you all keep a secret? Not just from your dad but from *everyone?* If this is going to work you can't tell a single soul." All heads nodded earnestly. Kelly bent down to whisper, "It's a boy. You're going to have a baby brother."

Excited squeals rose from the girls and a huge grin broke out across Randall's face. The children all began to talk at once. "Shh!" Kelly admonished. "Remember. Absolute secrecy."

"We're good at secrets," Tammy said, and when Kelly cocked her head skeptically, the little girl reminded her, "You and Daddy didn't know we planned your ceremony."

Kelly laughed. "True. Okay, I trust you. And now…" She straightened to see her husband a little way off, love lighting his eyes as he held out his hand to her. "Max is waiting for me."

HARLEQUIN *Super* ROMANCE®

WHITE KNIGHT INVESTIGATIONS

A new series by M.J. Rodgers

Meet the Knight brothers,
David, Jack, Richard and Jared—
Silver Valley, Washington's finest
detectives. They're ready and
willing to help anyone who calls!

Baby by Chance
(#1116 March 2003)

Susan Carter needs to find the
man who fathered her unborn
child. In desperation she turns to
David Knight. She knows she's
going to look bad—she doesn't
even know the man's last name—
but she has no other choice.

For the Defense
(#1137 June 2003)

Jack Knight isn't used to having to
justify himself to anyone, and that's
exactly what lawyer Diana Mason is
demanding he do. He's not the
Knight she wants working for her,
but he's the only one who can prove
her client is innocent of murder.

*Available wherever
Harlequin books are sold.*

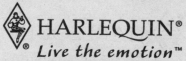

HARLEQUIN®
Live the emotion™

Visit us at www.eHarlequin.com

HSRWKI2T

HARLEQUIN *Super*ROMANCE®

Everybody in New Skye comes to Charlie's Carolina Diner. Join them in this six-book series as they meet old friends and new loves, reminisce about their past and plan their futures!

The Ballad of Dixon Bell
by Lynnette Kent
(Harlequin Superromance #1118)

Dixon Bell has loved Kate Bowdrey for as long as he can remember. Now that she's available again, he's coming home to New Skye to make all his dreams come true. There's only one thing stopping him—L. T. LaRue, Kate's soon-to-be ex-husband, one of the most powerful men in town.

Available in March 2003
wherever Harlequin books are sold.

Watch for the third book
in the AT THE CAROLINA DINER series
in August 2003.

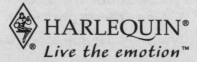

HARLEQUIN®
Live the emotion™

Visit us at www.eHarlequin.com

HSRCDLK

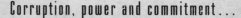
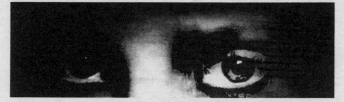

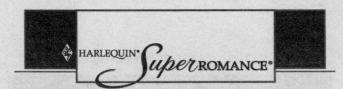

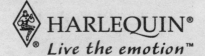